1

First of All

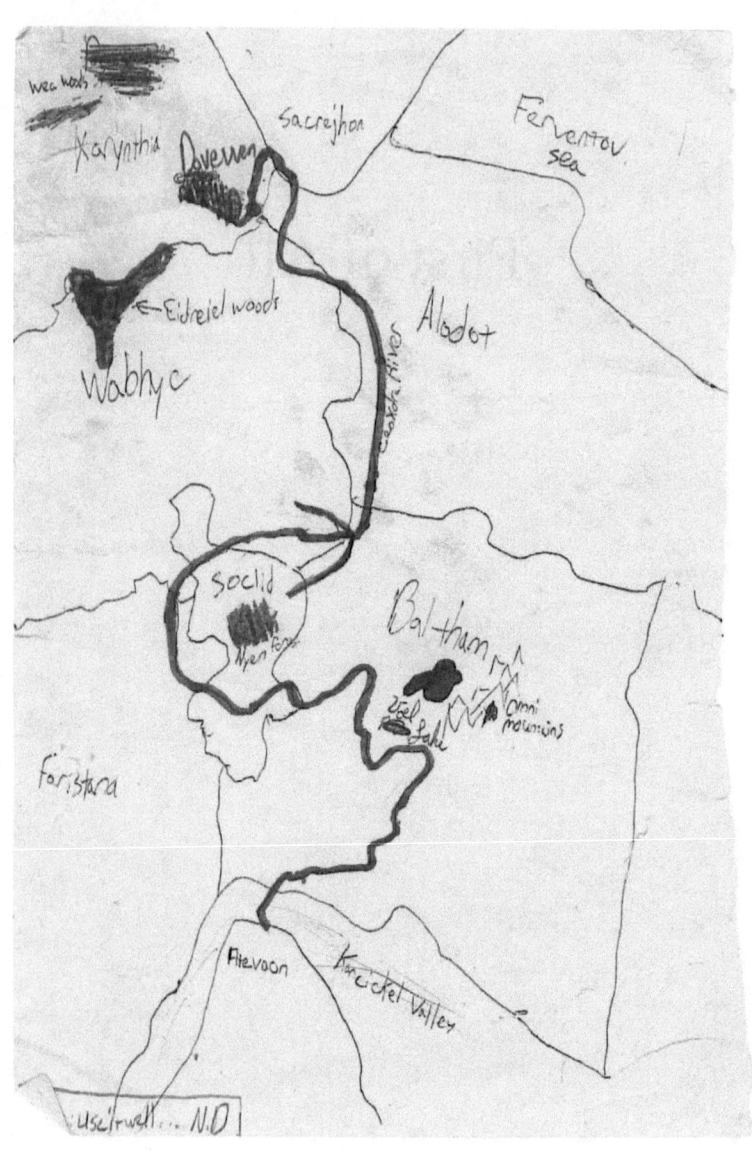

4

The Heptology of The Seven Golden Chairs
Book One

First of All

Written by H.T. Wilson

Lulu Publishers

To:

My brother and sister for our fun,
imaginative, and crazy times that never
end!

My parents who, in everything they do,
encourage me to strive to the sky's
limit!

My friends that I made throughout my
lifetime and anymore I will make.

Most of all, I give the biggest, most
enormous thanks to my Savior, Jesus
Christ, who gave me this gift to write
to you all in his name.

Thanks!
H.T.W

1

Everything was silent. A light crept around. The tone
would make a snap of a finger sound like someone yelling
in your young soft ears until your eardrums fell out! The
light wasn't an object or a person. It was a spirit that was
light, so bright that boulders and mountains would crack as
it walked.

"It is time," He said.

Out of those thundering words, water came rippling
and dripping out. The first tree grew to its adult size at the
end of the sentence. The sun grew in humbleness. It bowed
its beautiful red hair and then did what was commanded of
it. At last, the birds started to sing and the fish raced in
water. The soil, grass, and rocks came up from
underground. He used some of the rocks to make
mountains. Among all of them, two were very special.

One was at the south of the land. Lava spewed out of it like a pot of boiling water. It was pitch black compared to all the other mountains of our world. In the north was a mountain made of pure gold. It shone in the day and night. To put him in that beautiful snow-peaked mountain would make it shine even more!

In the mountain of the north, he had seven beautiful golden chairs carved and embedded with diamonds. Only He knew the people who would sit there. They were the ones who would help his people when they were in jeopardy. They had been chosen for that particular job before they were even born!

That reminded him of another job he had to do -- make his people. He lifted his powerful hands into the air. Dust and leaves swirled around the world and a massive amount of people appeared.

The people from Faristana are fairies. The girl fairies are simply called "Fairies." They dress in a deep pink or a royal purple. They have wings as delicate as a butterfly's. Male fairies are called "Fardons." They dress in a deep green or blue. Their wings are stronger and they possess and hold a stronger magical force than the girls. That is why the Fardons are the only ones allowed to go to war. The Fairies hold regular, thin magic, such as granting a small wish or disappearing for a few seconds, things of that sort. The loss of a fairy's wings is like dealing with death itself or a heart torn in two. The fairies have a power, but I will not tell you about it now. Why should I? It would ruin the fantastic surprise!

Soclidans have fiery red hair. They have pale skin and a magical power you will soon learn. I will tell you about the Wabhycs, the Alodotians, and the Xarynthians during my story.

In Xarynthia, a family believed in The Creator. They went to the north to Sacrejhon, the mountain He stays on, to talk to him. The parents, Mayla, who was from Soclid, and Sade, who was from Xarynthia, had their first baby -- a boy they named Ashin. They took the baby boy on his first trip to Sacrejhon. That is where The Creator put his hand on the back of the boy's neck and a birthmark appeared. The birthmark was that of a golden sword with a purple handle. As he touched the boy, Ashin opened his eyes and smiled. The Creator knew he was one of the favored.

~~~~~~

Ashin thought about what his parents told him about that day while he absentmindedly rubbed the back of his neck.

"What's that on the back of your neck, Ashin?" Kedin spoke slightly louder. "Is it used to chop off your own sickly, brainless head?"

Other boys snickered around him as Ashin buried his head in his own arms, covering the birthmark. "Ooh, can I have it?" another asked derisively.

"Shut up, boys! You have plenty of work to get done!" their teacher scolded.

"It wasn't my fault!" Kedin mocked a puppy's plea. "Ashin was trying to show off his stupid birthmark!"

"Liar!" Ashin lunged at him.

"Stop!" ordered the teacher, getting between them. The teacher returned to the front of the room. Kedin looked around, then poked Ashin in the back of his neck.

"Ouch!" Ashin yelped.

Ashin was in the Elbroc School for Boys. His school was named after the first king of Xarynthia. The king had no history because the world had just begun a mere sixty years before.

"Nyvon created our written language just last month," his teacher declared. "Now we can learn to communicate in that written language instead of pictures."

Ashin sat up, his interest piqued. He looked at his best friend, Doshan, and raised his eyebrows. The only reason they were best friends was because they were both biracial. Doshan's mother was a Fairy and Ashin's mother was a Soclidan. The edge of Ashin's short hair was red. He didn't look like his mom, but he had her power! Doshan was the same way, but he had Fardon power, while his mom had only Fairy power.

In the middle of her sentence, the teacher stopped to look at the sun because they didn't have clocks. The sun was in the middle of the sky. She cleared her throat. "Class dismissed."

The boys scrambled out of the school like eggs in a frying pan. As Ashin was exiting, somebody grabbed his shirt. He knew without looking who it was -- Kedin.

"Hey, Ashin, why don't you go to Mixed-Up Land? This land is not called Soclixar. It is only for pure Xarynthians," Kedin taunted.

Ashin rolled his eyes. "Well, pure Xarynthians don't have powers."

With those words, the fight was on. Kedin swung in anger. His fist hit Ashin's cheek. Ashin swung back, punching Kedin in the temple. It was getting rough. Kedin was good at punching, but Ashin's legs were stronger. Kedin punched him in his nose. Ashin kicked Kedin in the stomach, then tripped him. It wasn't Ashin's fault that his mom had been forced into marriage! He got on top of Kedin and put his knee on Kedin's stomach. A boy Ashin didn't know came between them as Kedin was gulping for air. Ashin was pulled away from Kedin. Ashin's bloody nose ran like a waterfall.

"We've got to get out of here!" Doshan warned.

The boys ran down the street with Kedin right on their heels. They turned left into an alley, then made a quick right turn. Doshan ran to his adobe house.

"Bye, Ashin," Doshan called out.

Ashin waved goodbye and continued running. Kedin quickened his steps. He was only an arm's length away. Ashin ran into the Wea Woods, which everyone referred to as the "Double W," ducking and dodging the trees' grasp. Ashin hid behind a boulder watching Kedin, who was near the edge of the woods. He looked around, but he didn't see Ashin. He left clutching his bruised stomach.

A tree picked up Ashin by his legs. "Oh, look what we've got here... a human child!" said the tree. "He is not supposed to be in this cursed land, I'll bet."

Ashin swung his legs back and forth trying to touch the tree's bark. Back and forth... back and forth. Ashin swung his body until he started to get dizzy, but he knew he had to focus. Finally, he touched the bark. The tree released Ashin as it was swallowed up by flames. Ashin scrambled to his feet and left the home of these wicked trees.

Panting, Ashin went inside his house. He was exhausted from his ordeal. His mom, Mayla, was outside doing the laundry. Her red hair danced in the wind. She walked through the open door and greeted him. "Hey, Ashin!" When she saw the dried blood on his nose, she stepped back to grab a wet towel.

"You fought him again," she said quietly.

"Yes, him," he mumbled.

"Look, this can't continue to be done secretly. One day it will spill out that you have been fighting Kedin. You could be expelled from school!"

"I know," he replied flatly, "but I had to defend myself!"

Mayla sighed. "Your father used to say fire continues the fire, but water extinguishes it."

Ashin hated thinking about his father. Suddenly, the painful vivid images came back like a dog hunting him down, wanting to tear him to pieces. His dad had died during the summer floods two years ago. It was a horrible memory watching his dad drown and to be unable to help him. The worst thing was seeing his father's limp body floating in the muddy water.

Ashin pushed the thought of his father aside. Right now his stomach needed attention. He ate some thick, delicious cheese soup that had herbs mixed in it. He tore off some bread and ate it with the soup.

After Ashin had finished eating, he laid down on his cot. He tried to stay awake and think about the events that had occurred earlier in the day. *I did it for a reason*, he thought in his own defense. *Anyway, he got the first punch, right? Or do words count?* He drifted far away from reality until he was sleeping like a baby.

~~~~~~

The next day was a regular school day. Ashin nibbled like a mouse on some bread left over from the previous night's dinner and stuffed the rest in his cloth sack. He put on his *lliwani,* a pale brown tunic, much like a robe with pants that stops at the ankle. Ashin put on his sandals and left for school. His stomach churned as he wondered if his teacher had seen the fight. If she had, what would be his punishment? Ashin pondered those questions really hard.

"Ashin, wait up!" a voice called out. It was Doshan. Ashin stopped. "Guess what?" Doshan said when he'd caught up.

"What?"

"I'm moving to Soclid!"

Ashin was surprised. He thought that if Doshan's family ever moved, it would be to Faristana, where his mom had come from. Ashin donned a fake smile and said, "Wow! Cool!"

Deep down inside of his heart, he didn't feel that way. It meant he would have to make another friend and it was very rare to find a biracial person in Xarynthia. Ashin wanted a friend he could relate to -- someone like himself.

All of the kids were playing outside of the school when he arrived. Kedin smirked when he saw Ashin. The teacher, Vena Pelced, opened the door. Somehow she already knew he was outside. Her face was firm. Her stare could make you feel like a molecule of dust against a mighty wind. Ashin gulped and walked forward. He knew what this was about.

"Good luck," Doshan whispered.

Ms. Pelced slammed the door behind him and cleared her throat. "I saw you and Kedin fighting yesterday, but I only saw the middle of it. I talked to Kedin earlier today and he said you used your powers."

"I did not!" Ashin wailed. "Don't you even trust me anymore?"

"Your father was respected by all and you are like him, so to answer your question, I do trust your word. I do expect better behavior from you, though. Your father loved The Creator. You act like you've never met The Creator, nor seen his face." Her voice grew louder, like thunder rolling through the sky. Ashin's heart sped up, pounding hard. He clinched his teeth and slightly shook his head before she continued.

"I'm sure that one touch from The Creator told you everything… what to do and what not to do. You certainly keep your grades up, but if we were to grade you on your self-control and your rude horrendous mouth, you would fail! Although Kedin insulted you first, or whatever happened, why did you have to hit him? You are not showing me that your family ever knew The Creator."

Ms. Pelced grabbed a blank sheet of white paper and jotted something down in pictography at the speed of light. She handed the paper to him. "Here, give this to your mom. I am expelling you for the rest of the school year!" She stood up and said in a soft voice, "You need to learn someday."

Ashin just nodded and opened the door. He saw the kids who were right by the door and back by the wall step back quickly. They snickered and whispered to each other while staring at him as he walked past them. Suddenly, jumping out from nowhere was Kedin. He scared Ashin out of his wits! "Boo!"

Everyone started laughing. Ashin ran into the Dovevven Forest that was only a mile from where he was standing. He ran until he was at the bank of the Ceoxdra River. He sat down on the grass, taking in the scent of the water, both fresh and fishy at the same time. Ashin took a quick glance at the sun to make sure he wouldn't be late getting home. The rushing river lulled him to sleep.

"Papa!" six year-old Ashin cried out in excitement. He'd caught his first fish! His dad swung him around to celebrate.

"Way to go! Mayla, do you have the bread and cheese?"

"Yes." His mother's smile was like the sun. She sat in a lady-like posture in the grass. Sade winked at his wife, then went on playing with Ashin. The boy ran hand-in-hand with his father, laughing and chuckling about every trip and fall. Ashin looked at his father strangely. He seemed to be fading away from life.

"Dad! Dad!" Ashin yelled. He was frightened. "Where are you?" For a second, everything went black.

"Son! Son!" he heard his father frantically call out.

The sound of raging water was heard and then he saw everything again. Ashin was a year older.

"Run, Ashin, run!" his mother screamed. Her clothes, *llanas*, were soaked.

The waves were flooding the forest. Ashin looked back at his dad, trying to survive. His mom pushed Ashin out of the way as she held onto a tree. There were tears streaming down her cheeks. Her hair stuck to her face like strings.

"We can't help you, Sade! I'm sorry!" The word 'sorry' echoed around the forest as his father yelled with his last breath.

Ashin woke up, springing up from the grass. He was panting and his heart was breathing very fast. His eyes were wide with fear. He looked up into the sky. It was navy blue. The clouds covered the moon, granting his wish for the closest-to-no-light as possible. Ashin knew he had to use his powers to find his way back home.

He turned his hand into fire. He took one step at a time to make sure he wasn't catching a tree or anything else flammable on fire. Crickets chirped their loudest song. Owls hooted a few times, not many, but enough to scare the daylights out of somebody when it was deadly quiet. After an hour, he found himself safe at home.

He entered the house as quietly as he could. From the wooden counters to the pans and pots, the house was empty. In the living room, there was only a wooden couch and sitting on it was his mom.

"Where were you?" she questioned when he came into the room.

"I…uh…well…" Ashin stammered.

Mayla looked up from her knitting and saw the smoke gently rising from his fingertips. Her mouth curved into a sly smile. "I can see you got home safe." She said nothing more on that subject. "Doshan told me you received a letter from your teacher about being expelled."

"What?" That was the closest Ashin could get without actually screaming.

"Don't be mad at him. If you wouldn't tell me, who would?"

Yeah, he sure is my best friend! Ashin thought sarcastically.

Ashin was walking towards his room when his mom said, "You won't find your bed in there. I set it on fire because we're moving to Soclid with Doshan's family."

"Yes!" In an instant Ashin seemed to forget all his worries or that he was mad at Doshan. They were moving away from this raggedy old trash heap!

"We can't bring everything with us, so I had to burn it. We're leaving tomorrow."

2

"Yeks, come here now!" The voice was sharp and commanding. It was too dark to see who it was. Not one speck of light was able to cast the tiniest shadow of the setting.

"Yes, my master," a squeaky voice answered. Feet quiet as a little mouse's crept into the room.

"Has Veil found any of the other ones yet?"

"No, my master," was the quick response.

"We have only one out of seven. If I don't get all of them, I will kill you first, then you will be mine, forever chained to do all that I say!"

"Yes... my master," the voice said slowly.

The feet that had come in so fast before were now as slow as a snail. Yeks went into a different room. The only light was from a foggy crystal ball and a pair of eyes staring at him.

They were white, like a snowflake before it lands on a salivating tongue. No pupils were visible.

"Yeks, I already told you, I'm not using the ten wishes because after all ten are used, I die. They are supposed to be used only for an emergency," a lady's deep voice rang out.

"But Veil," Yeks protested, "my life is at stake!"

"I don't care whether you live or die," was her flat response.

"Master, may I go outside?" Veil asked. She said it like a question in order to let her have some authority and leave him some.

"Go ahead."

She went outside wearing a hooded cloak. She pulled it down revealing her charcoal skin and pure black, shoulder-length hair. Obviously frightened, Yeks stroked his long, gray beard and started playing with it.

Veil rubbed a tall tree at the bottom of its pale brown barked trunk, then stood up. "It is time."

Ice gradually climbed up the tree to the top. The whole tree froze and shattered.

~~~~~~

The next morning, Ashin and his mother dragged their bags of clothes, a few of Ashin's toys, and some clay pots and pans outside, then loaded the belongings on their mule before departing for Doshan's house. Ashin knocked softly on the door and Doshan opened it. He tried not to look exuberant because he was still mad from the other day, but Ashin couldn't help jumping for joy!

"I can't believe this! I'm finally going to Soclid!" Ashin's face stared dreamily into space.

"Me neither," Doshan finally responded.

Mayla unrolled her cot and that of her son in Doshan's family's living room. Ashin and Doshan went outside to play.

"You got the bows and arrows?" Ashin inquired.

"Yeah, and the bull's eye," Doshan replied with a smile.

The games began. They started as the boys focused their eyes on the little blood-red circles in the middle of the bull's eye. The boys laughed and jumped around, shooting the arrows from different angles. Ashin climbed mid-way up a tree. His legs hugged it as he laid back until he was upside down, focusing. He shot the arrow. It flew past Doshan and landed right above the red circle. Doshan looked awestruck.

"That was awesome!"

The sun seemed to fall down from the sky. The blues, grays, yellows, oranges, and whites mixed into the sky, making the scenery beautiful. The boys knew it was time to go in.

~~~~~~

"Mom, what was Soclid like before you left and married Dad?" Ashin asked from his bed.

Mayla got up wearily. "It was another sun! Somebody was making a fire if it wasn't you. Everybody greeted you warmly. There was no pressure against you. The Ceoxdra River near Soclid looked like melted pure gold, running like a cheetah; then, just like a cheetah, it slows down after catching its prey. Its prey is winter! Cool, huh?"

"Mom, what's your favorite color?" he asked suddenly.

"Red. The dominant favorite colors in Soclid are red, yellow, and orange." Mayla always had to explain something all the way through. She loved to talk. "I believe you might fit in because your favorite color is yellow, eh?"

"Yeah."

The next morning, both families led their mules, luggage, and bags into a colossal, thin wooden sailing barge. The boat gleamed with a shining coat of snow white paint. Even though it seemed massive, it was like a baby white roach teetering-tottering through the mouth of a wide, sparkling river.

Mayla handed the guard a bag of copper coins and he let her pass through to the bottom deck where all the animals were stowed. There were many other people on that deck, crowding around as if looking for something. Mayla set the food bag down in a corner, then sat down beside it. Ashin was on the top deck with Doshan. The boat started to move out into the center of the Ceoxdra River.

24

Wow! Goodbye, Xarynthia! Ashin felt free as a bird. The Ceoxdra River crossed through all of the countries, so during the voyage Ashin would be able to see what other people looked like! He decided to explore the boat. It looked very cheap with dishwater-colored bed sheets serving as sails. *This boat couldn't last a minute in a storm!*

Absentmindedly, Ashin bumped into someone. "Hello, young fellow!" he heard a low, smooth voice say. Ashin looked up. A bald man with a very short beard was staring down at him.

"Hi," Ashin responded quietly, backing away. "I'm sorry I bumped into you, sir."

"No problem. I see you're interested in this ship." Ashin nodded. "I'll tell you what… I'll give you a copper coin each day if you'll come help me load luggage and to sell things and clean up around here. We really need workers around here."

Ashin was delighted about the offer he'd been given, but he knew there was one thing he'd have to do before he could accept. "I have to ask my mom first."

"Okay, go ahead."

Ashin ran down to the bottom deck and told his mom about the man's offer. "Sure! We need the money for food!" she said.

Ashin was quickly put to work, mopping dirty floors and when the boat stopped to collect passengers and sell things, there was Ashin, unloading the heavy wooden crates. He couldn't wait to get to other ports to see how the people from each country looked. He saw people from a

Wabhyc tribe with their charcoal skin and glowing white eyes with no visible pupil. They also have a special kind of power. There were beautiful Alodot people from another country–mortals with pale skin. The Alodot girls have fair hair and blue eyes; no matter what their age, the boys have either sandy or dusty hair color and blue eyes.

The boat crossed the country of Baltham during its long journey. Those people looked normal--medium to wide eyes and both genders had pure white hair, but their ears with pointed tips were unusual. They have the ability either to move things or to stop things from moving with their magnetic force and they also have the power to heal minor wounds.

Ashin got off the small boat he'd been unloading as the sky had grown cloudy. *I'd better hurry,* he cautioned himself. Before he knew it, the rain began to drizzle down, then the raindrops became much larger, pelting him like rocks. Ashin ran back to the barge as the wind blew harder and harder. *This isn't a natural storm. I know it!*

Everyone began to panic and scream as the wind ripped one of the sails apart. "Somebody mend that thing!" the captain roared over the sound of the pounding rain. Many people started to climb up the rigging to obey his command, but could do nothing as they were not equipped to make the repair, having neither a needle nor strong thread. The wind pushed Ashin to the deck. He struggled to get up, but his legs were shaking. He tried again, but was pushed down by the force of the boat turning the opposite way.

"Turn it around, you fool! Move out of my way. I'll steer it since you're too busy panicking!" The captain seized control to guide the ship.

26

A lightning bolt hit the ship, ignited, and the flames started to spread like the wind scattering seeds everywhere. All of the people from the lower decks ran to the top deck to hear what the captain was going to do. Crewmen lowered small lifeboats which carried five passengers in each one. They had only ten lifeboats--not enough for everyone on the ship.

"Children and women first!" the captain yelled.

Ashin felt a hand on his shoulder. "There you are." It was his mom. Mayla and Ashin waited in line to board a lifeboat. Ashin's heart pounded as he watched the seventh lifeboat being filled. *Now I wish I'd have stayed in Xarynthia!*

The eighth and ninth boats were being filled at the same time. The flames were spreading fast and the water level was up to Ashin's knees. People felt the barge slowly sinking, but they tried to stay calm and wait for another boat. The tenth boat was ready to be filled. Doshan and his parents got into the boat. There was another person in front of Ashin and Mayla. Ashin's chin quivered. *I am going to die!*

"Wait! Wait! Don't lower the boat," Doshan yelled as he scrambled out of the lifeboat. He looked at Ashin and his mother. "Get in."

"Are you serious?"

"Yeah."

"Thank you very much!"

27

Doshan shrugged. "No problem. I took swimming lessons for times like this. Now go on, before they get impatient."

Ashin never thought about what a good friend he had until he was faced with death.
"Thanks," he repeated, scrambling into the boat.

"Abandon ship!" the captain yelled. Everyone dived into the water just as the deck gave way behind them. The people in the lifeboats were rowing as fast as they could towards the nearest land. The churning water splashed on everyone, soaking them with ice-cold water.

Come on! Come on! You're almost there! Ashin thought to himself. He wanted to get to land as soon as possible. Finally, they made it to a shore. Ashin hurried to get out. Doshan and the other swimmers made it to shore almost as quickly as the boats.

As soon as everyone was on dry land, the captain announced, "Listen up, people! Tomorrow we will continue the trip to Soclid, but we will have to buy another boat. Is anyone interested in helping with the finances?" He squirmed as he said the last word. His face turned red because he looked uncomfortable having to ask them for money.

Ashin got up, reached into his pocket, and pulled out the pouch which contained the coins he had earned, then handed it to the captain.

"Thank you, son," the captain whispered. At that moment, others started to add a copper coin or two to Ashin's pouch. Soon it was full. "This is more than enough," said the captain. He looked at Ashin, then everyone else. "Thank you, so much... all of you. I'll go find the nearest village to find out where we are, if we're close to Soclid... and see if there are any boats for sale."

The faces in the crowd showed a mixture of fear, hope, and anxiety. A tiny smile lit Ashin's face. He closed his eyes for a little while, but soon fell asleep.

~~~~~~

"Ashin, wake up!" Hands furiously shook him. As he slowly opened his eyes, he saw his mom's face, beaming with excitement.

"What's going on?" he mumbled.

"The captain found a boat!" Mayla practically screamed! "Everyone is loading up. We'd better hurry!" She ran over to get in line. Ashin smiled. He hadn't seen his mom this happy in a long time. Ashin scrambled up and followed her.

One by one, every got aboard the boat, painted a rich, creamy blue. When Ashin was about to step onto the boat, he knocked on it. *Way sturdier than the first one!* He and his mom went below, where Mayla found a place to sit, but Ashin had to explore the boat and see its cool features. He went on the top deck and took a deep breath smelling the air, clean after the rain. The water danced and roared as it rolled ships down it's majestic river. Ashin saw something out of the corner of his left eye. He quickly turned around as fiery blasts of light shot up into the sky. Ashin gasped in awe at the sight as he watched the clouds turn to yellowish-red. Mayla ran up to the top deck. There were tears streaming from her eyes. She put her hands over her mouth and screamed.

"Ladies and gentlemen, we are coming up on the docks of Criam, Soclid," the captain announced over the loud speaker.

At last! Ashin sighed. He looked at the village. *Soclid!* He couldn't believe he was finally here! The boat slowed down to a stop. Everyone ran out as soon as the gangplank was in place. So much had happened. They were glad to be at their destination.

"Mama! Papa!" Mayla cried out as she ran up to her parents, hugging them tightly.

"*Elko la neio*, Mayla. Welcome home," her mother said in a deep, raspy voice. "And who is this?"

"Mama, meet Ashin, my son."

"Oh, so this is my grandson? Come on, give your grandmamma a hug."

Ashin was the same height as his stout grandmother. His grandmother had rose red- colored eyes that shaped into a perfect horizon. Her short, pale red hair, streaked with gray, looked a little wild, as if it hadn't been combed for days. Ashin hugged her and his grandfather.

As Mayla, Ashin, and Mayla's parents walked down the busy street, Ashin turned to see all of the sights -- people with many different types of red hair and eyes, even some with freckles! The skin tones of skin ranged from a light tan to the palest of white. There was a lot of action going on in the city. School was just letting out and kids were bustling about... trading, buying and selling, everything was happening so fast, no one knew if they'd gotten ripped off or didn't get their product!

Ashin noticed a huge house on the left side of the street, just before they left the rowdy side of town. It was not tall, but it was very wide and long! Wood planks painted red were lined up horizontally a few yards away from the front door which served as a fence, which stretched the length of least three houses.

Mayla's parents, Savov and Qana, opened the door of the unusual house and led them inside. Ashin gasped at the sight of all of the people waiting inside. Mayla's older brother Wexot, his wife Yayah, and their two kids, Navion and Jalia, were there, as well as Mayla's younger sister Kota and her husband Eter. Finally, the whole family was together.

The next morning, Ashin's stomach churned like butter. He was going off to his new school. He put on his new bold royal red *lliwani* that he'd bought at a nearby store. He stuffed his mouthful of bread and venison, then headed off to school.

He saw Doshan talking with three boys who appeared to be the same age or maybe a little older. *Hey, who's Doshan talking to?* He wondered. Ashin stared at them, but kept his distance. Doshan glanced at him and gave him a quick smile.

A middle-aged man with conspicuously thick red hair announced, "School is in session, let's begin." The three boys ran ahead. Doshan strolled so that Ashin could catch up with him.

"What was that all about?" Ashin asked him, putting a slight inflection on the word "about."

Doshan ignored the question except to say, "I'll tell you after school," then gave him a mysterious smile. His curiosity left unsatisfied, Ashin groaned.

To Ashin it seemed that when school started, it felt like it was never going to end! His teacher, the middle-aged man with the striking red hair and hoarse voice slurred his words, making everything seem to move in slow motion. *What are they talking about?* He tried to answer the teacher's question, but it made his head hurt even more! Finally, the bell rang and school was out for the day.

Once outside, he caught up with Doshan. "Now will you tell me?"

"No."

"But this morning you said…"

Doshan sighed. "I'm going to let *them* tell you, but we first have to get there."

"Where's there?"

"Follow me. We're going through the Nyen forest."

Ashin moaned. His feet were aching, but they kept moving. He was anxious to see what this was all about! Daylight was being snared by the approaching night.

"Don't try to use your powers now," Doshan commanded. Ashin looked at his friend, thinking, *I hope you're doing the right thing.*

Ashin wasn't watching where he was going and tripped over a boulder. "Ouch!" he yelped.

"Shh!"

The leaves of a bush rustled. Doshan moved over to the boulder that Ashin had tripped over, pounded on it two times, tapped the grass a couple of times, then pounded the boulder one last time. The boulder magically moved aside, revealing a tunnel to Doshan's secret place.

"Go in."

Ashin held his breath and stepped into the tunnel unaware that an adventure of a lifetime awaited him!

3

J ust as the two best friends stepped down to the
surface of the tunnel, a kerosene lamp was lighted and
beside it three boys were waiting -- the same ones Ashin
had seen with Doshan earlier that day! They gave Doshan a
quick nod and a slight handshake. The boy with wings
glared at Ashin.

"Ashin is my friend," Doshan declared hastily.

"What's going on?" asked Ashin for what seemed
like the hundredth time that day.

The winged boy cleared his throat. "We noticed
your friend was biracial from his unusually pale skin and
deep brown Xarynthian hair, so we went to talk to him.
Two years ago we started a club called the Underground
Biracial Juveniles with Powers…UBJP for short. It's top
secret and only those of us in this room know about it.
Another requirement for membership is you must have an
unique birthmark. We learned your friend also has one."

"You do?" Ashin said, turning to Doshan. Doshan rolled up his left sleeve and there, near his shoulder, was an outline of a panther.

"Do you have one?" the winged one asked Ashin. Ashin showed them his birthmark, then mouthed to Doshan, "Why didn't you tell me?" Doshan shrugged.

The boy pointed to himself. "I'm Darclep." He pointed to a boy beside him who had orange hair. The color was more red-orange than yellow-orange -- a good balance. "This is Rief and behind me is our leader, Somolo."

Somolo stepped out of the darkness. His pure white hair stood out from his head, which was smaller than his large body. He was only a bit taller than Ashin. Darclep also had white hair, a common Balthamian trait. Ashin could tell that Darclep was also part Faristanian.

"How old are you?" Rief asked, breaking the silence.

"Nine." Doshan and Ashin answered at the same time. They learned that Somolo was thirteen, Darclep was twelve, and Rief was eleven.

"Follow me." Somolo commanded and started into the tunnel, which quickly became more and more narrow. Soon there was only enough room to wiggle their way through. Dust began to fall like rain. *I wonder if I'm claustrophobic.* Ashin thought he could hear his own heart beat. It was slow, like a that of a turtle carrying a boulder on its back.

Darclep touched a stone and just like the other one, it magically moved. *He moved the other stone when we came in here! Cool!*

The tunnel ended as they entered a massive arena. They stopped to draw straws; Somolo drew the short one. "This is going to be too easy," he mumbled under his breath.

"What are we doing?" Doshan asked.

"Before you enter UBJP, we have to see if you are good enough, so we're going to fight. Somolo got the shortest straw, so he gets to pick his challenger."

Somolo studied the boys. "I choose the boy who has tinted red hair on the top of his head and a birthmark on his neck shaped like a sword -- Ashin!" Ashin's eyes turned from brown to red. A force pulled him forward. It was time. *So that's his power...okay.*

Somolo lifted his hands and like a rag doll Ashin went into the air. Ashin felt his heart surge into his throat. His heart squeezed tightly, then suddenly, the force was gone. Somolo grinned as Ashin fell bottom first to the ground. Rief and Darclep started to laugh. Ashin clenched his teeth. *Full power!*

Fire flashed from Ashin's hands toward Somolo. Screams of agony came from Ashin's challenger's mouth. Somolo's friends watched in awe. Ashin turned to Doshan and smiled. Doshan gave him a thumbs up.

Somolo was panting when Ashin stopped the fire. He healed in less than a second. "Wow! That was awesome! I'm not used to getting beat that bad!"

37

"Thanks," Ashin replied. "How did you do that?"

"What?"

"You know, do your healing thing."

"Oh, I use my power to heal myself. I can't do that when facing death, though." Somolo explained.

"My vote is this little boy is in!" Darclep shouted proudly. Ashin nodded, trying to seem to be humble, but he couldn't hide how happy he felt!

It was Doshan's turn. Rief was his opponent. Doshan swung and missed. Rief kicked him in the side of his head, knocking him down to the ground. Bolts of fire were shot at Doshan…or what was thought to *be* Doshan. A three-second earthquake struck, surprising everyone. Rief tripped and the fire from his hands stopped. Doshan was nowhere to be seen. Rief's head was turned violently and he was bent over backwards. Rief fell to the ground as a burst of electricity flashed through his body, momentarily leaving him in a state of shock.

"I can't wait to see how you are with your wings," Darclep commented. "You'll be unstoppable!"

"Thanks," said Doshan, beaming.

"Meet us here early tomorrow, then again at night," Somolo commanded. "Is that clear?"

"Sir, yes, sir!" Doshan joked.

Ashin and Doshan went back to the point where they came in. Darclep moved the stone, and they started for home. They failed to notice a pair of eyes watching them… pure white eyes.

~~~~~~

"Yeks!"

"I'm here, master."

"You're going on a little journey… for the jewels." A demonic voice pierced the darkness.

"Yes, my master."

"And you won't come back here until you find all six of them."

"Agreed."

Yeks left the mountain Htevaon and made his way down into Karcickel valley. He looked at the black mountain spewing lava out all sides and sighed. "I guess it's time to start digging."

~~~~~~

"Where is he?" Mayla wondered.

Ashin was nowhere to be found. Worse yet, Lya, Doshan's mom, hadn't seen Doshan since that morning. Wexot, Yayah, Kota, and Eter were all searching for Ashin. A river of tears flowed down Mayla's beautiful face. She would never be able to get over it if Ashin died… if he was dead. Whenever she saw Ashin, she was reminded of Sade. She couldn't lose both of them. She sobbed uncontrollably.

Eter came over to where Mayla was sitting. "Have you found him?" Eter asked in his crusty voice.

"No."

"I'm going to look in the Nyen Forest. Hopefully he's there," said Eter, then mumbled, "alive."

Now alone, Mayla whispered, "Come back to us, Ashin... please come back."

~~~~~~

"That was awesome!" Ashin exclaimed.

"I can't believe both of us made it into the...UBJP!" They said in unison.

"Ashin, is that you?" a voice called out.

Uh oh. Ashin thought. A figure came towards him. It was Uncle Eter and he didn't look happy.

"What were you thinking?" Eter asked, shaking him. "Your mother is worried sick. Answer me! Where have you been?"

"I...I... was just playing with Doshan in the Nyen forest," Ashin lied.

"This late at night?" Eter gripped both boys' arms tightly and dragged them home. "I wonder what Mayla will say about this,"

It felt as if they were walking for miles, but finally they were at the big house. "Look who I found in the Nyen forest," Eter announced loudly.

Everybody in the house, including Mayla, turned around to see both boys standing there, looking sheepish. Mayla was livid. She grabbed Ashin and dragged him into his room. Ashin took a step back, but it was too late. His mom slapped him hard. It happened so quickly, he was in shock. His mother never hit him. She usually made him work off his punishments, but she never hit him!

Ashin's eyes welled up with tears, then one by one rolled down his cheek. He said nothing, but his eyes said it all. He was hurt…but not physically.

Mayla left the room and closed it, leaving him to cry and think about what he'd done. He didn't know people would be looking for him… or did he?

A little later, Mayla came back in, still wearing the stern, uninviting look on her face. "What were you doing?"

"I was playing with Dosh--"

"Stop lying to me, boy!" Mayla snapped. She was exhausted! "I've decided that you're not allowed to go into the Nyen forest at night."

Ashin was about to protest, but he knew that if he did, he would tell his mother everything and he was told to keep the UBJP a secret, so he just nodded in reply.

When Mayla left the room, Ashin laid on his cot and soon fell into a deep slumber.

"Daddy!" three year-old Ashin called out.

Nine year-old Ashin watched his younger self go up to the person he'd called 'Daddy.' It was too bright to see the face. The nine year-old Ashin was disgusted! The person touched the young Ashin's neck and there was the beginning of his birthmark. The young Ashin disappeared.

"Come here, son." Ashin shook his head.

"You're not my dad! You're not my dad!" He ran with all of his might. He blinked and saw that he was chained up. "Help! Help!" He saw the person look out of his window. "Dad, help me!" Ashin cried as he was dragged away from the person's house. The person walked away from his window.

"Nooooooo!"

Ashin opened his eyes and sprang out of bed. He looked out of the window. The sun was also climbing out of bed. Ashin dressed in some black new *lliwanis* and tiptoed out of his room.

Mom said I couldn't go at night, but she didn't say I couldn't go in the morning! Ashin thought.

He crept like a little ant to the door of the big house, then opened it slowly, hoping it wouldn't creak. He was a cheetah when he ran. He had to get there quickly and hoped Doshan was already there because there was no time to wait for him. He zigzagged through the Nyen Forest until he found the smooth gray stone. Ashin entered the password. "Pound. Pound. Tap. Tap. Pound."

Ladies first. A voice telepathed. Ashin jumped as a red and black blur dived into the tunnel ahead of him. *Uh oh. Will the boys kick me out? Who is this person?* A voice laughed in his mind. Ashin went into the tunnel. He didn't see anything, but he knew somebody was there.

"Ashin." He knew who *that* was.

"Hey, Doshan. You know, we're both late."

Doshan sighed. "I know."

Doshan closed the stone to the tunnel and followed Ashin. They went through the tunnel and out past the other stone that led to the massive arena. Darclep, Somolo, and Rief were a couple of feet away from the entrance when Doshan and Ashin came through. The three of them gasped, not at the sight of the two boys they'd met the day before, but because of the girl with the blood red hair and pupil-less white eyes right behind them!

~~~~~~

Yeks raised his hand and lightning flashed. He lowered them and heavy rain poured down. The precipitation grew greater and greater until it was as more than the storm he'd made a couple of years ago and the one earlier this year. Yeks flew over Doclazhec until he found a dull jewel in the range of his keen and discerning eyesight. He flew down to grab it, but an animal snapped its teeth at him! Yeks lunged at the animal, desperately grasping for the jewel. The animal jumped up as if protecting the jewel. Yeks wrestled the animal, but he was instantly pinned down to the ground. Yeks was able to get a closer look. The animal's dark gray eyes gave a heart-stabbing stare through the darkness. His face was like a bat's, his teeth the color of

43

mold. His body was as strong as the mountain lion, with a thin, scaly, very sharp tail. His mind set to tear up flesh.

"What do you want?" The breath of the animal smothered his face.

"The jewel." Yeks' breath came forcefully and exceedingly fast.

"For what? Your life?" The animal spoke like lightning itself.

"You really think I care about my life, Quutioy? I admit I do, but you have no choice in the matter. I have back up."

Immediately, the mud rose up and formed into hundreds of people. Quutioy took his paws off of Yeks and took many steps back. Yeks laughed as the Mudmen chained Quutioy. Yeks disappeared, but his malevolent laugh was still heard by Quutioy as he was buried alive in the mud.

~~~~~~~~~~~~~~~~~~~~~~~~~~~~~~~~~~~~~~

The girl's hair was down to her ribs. Her body type was thin. Her skin was coal black.

"Surprise!" she said, flinging her hands in the air. The boys fell silent. Not a movement was made. "I came to be a part of UBJP." Her voice was neither high nor low, but there was an edge to it.

Somolo glared at Doshan and Ashin. Doshan defended himself. "We didn't tell her anything."

"And?" the girl snapped. "I heard you talking in the forest. A secret reaches surface faster than a regular conversation."

Darclep sighed and whispered something to Somolo. Somolo looked disgusted, but he agreed with the plan. "Let's draw straws to see who fights her," said Darclep low voice. "Don't tell her about the birthmark stuff!"

"I'm waiting!" Iyaa shouted.

Darclep and Somolo slowly pulled two straws: long and long. "Yes!" They breathed a sigh of relief.

Rief drew his straw: long, then Ashin: short. *This is going to be too easy!* Ashin thought.

Seriously, I wouldn't be so sure of that! Your turn first and give it your best shot. *The thought transference... again.*

Large bolts of fire came towards the girl. Ashin stopped throwing the bolts after a few minutes. When the smoke and fire dissipated, the girl was still sitting there with her arms crossed, a bored look on her face. He threw more bolts of fire, but this time a black blur came towards him.

"The name's Iyaa and you're goin' down!" She kicked him in the stomach. "Oh, I'm sorry! Did that hurt?"

Ashin lunged at her, forcing the fight to the ground. He hit her in her right jaw, then the left. "I love the prideful ones. They're as arrogant as hyenas...only worse!"

Iyaa held Ashin's wrists and stood up. She dragged him until he also stood up. He tried to free his wrists, but her grip was like a steel trap. She slammed Ashin to the ground. He tried to get up, but she punched and kicked him until he clutched his stomach. Iyaa's fist was ready to hit. *No mercy.*

Ashin held his head low and forced the words out of his mouth, "Stop! I surrender!"

Iyaa smiled haughtily. "Didn't think you'd get beat by a girl, did you?" Ashin wondered why she always telepathed him. *Why didn't she just say it?*

"Wow, you can fight!" Rief commented.

Darclep turned to Ashin and Doshan. "One of you will have to get out of the UBJP because of this. Somolo and I will find out who it will be."

Ashin waited, looking nervously at Doshan who was biting his lip. Time crawled by. *We should be getting off to school now! Well, school can wait. I want to hear who's still in!*

"And the person who's out of UBJP is…" Darclep started to say. A huge pause melted in. Doshan and Ashin looked at each other. His stomach felt like it had been twisted a hundred times. "Doshan, you're out."

Doshan looked like he was going to cry, but he held it in and tried to take the bad news like a man…or so he thought. He nodded, then looked away from everybody.

Ashin kept his mouth shut tight. He wanted to stay in the UBJP. Iyaa smiled at Ashin, who glared back at her.

46

Her long red hair reminded him of his mother and he thought about what had happened the night before. Ashin went to Doshan and said, "We'll still see each other."

Doshan shook his head, ignoring Ashin's supposed sympathy. "No, it won't be the same. Bye."

"I'll hate you forever," Ashin mumbled under his breath as he his eyes settled on the triumphant girl.

Go ahead! She snarled back with a pugnacious attitude. *You're no match for me if you did want to fight!*

Ashin followed Doshan back to the entrance. "Bye Doshan," he said.

"Bye."

Ashin waited until Doshan was out of sight before turning back to the tunnel. He saw something he hadn't noticed before. A note was stabbed into the ground by a golden shining arrow. Ashin took the arrow and carefully picked up the note. He read the first line: "To the UBJP members." He hurried back inside to tell the others what he'd found.

4

"Darclep! Somolo! Rief!" Ashin cried out. "Look what I found!"

"Um, you seriously forgot someone. Are you mentally incapable to remember the smallest things?" Iyaa's face showed boredom.

Darclep ignored her statement. "We really should really be getting to school."

Ashin clasped his hands together. "Please let's read the note first!"

"Then you'll go to school?"

"Yeah!" Iyaa held back a laugh.

Mortified, Ashin gave the note to Darclep. "Okay, here's what it says."

Dear UBJP members,
I'm not an everyday client, but I need some help.
There are seven jewels that are scattered all over

Doclazhec. I really need them. Can you please find them for me? I don't care if it takes you a month, but if you're persistent, I say this job is good for you. The stones are a ruby, an emerald, a quartz, a sapphire, a diamond, a garnet, and a topaz. Please start as soon as possible.

PS. I will show my face to you when your journey is over and the time has come.

Somolo heard it all. "Let's meet up on the school grounds after school!"

Iyaa and Ashin ran to their part of the tall adobe-brick school. No one was outside, so they knew they were late. Ashin looked up in the sky. It was close to the middle of the sky which meant that school was almost out. Ashin turned around and saw Doshan sulking in the schoolyard. "Doshan, come here!" Ashin shouted.

Doshan simply ignored him, keeping his distance. *He's really my friend,* Doshan thought. *But he doesn't look sorry at all. I know he's happy. Maybe I'm not a good fighter. Maybe I should stick to what my dad is -- a blacksmith."*

Every "maybe" tugged and added more weight to Doshan's heart. Each one made him detest Ashin even more. Ashin's hair stood up every time somebody praised his acts. Maybe somebody needed to tell him he was arrogant once in a while!

Before they knew it, all of the kids came out. Ashin took one last look at Doshan, then went to see the UBJP members.

"Hey, Ashin!"

"Hey!" Ashin felt popular. He felt like he had a humongous number of friends now. Ashin ran up to Darclep, Rief, Somolo, and that disgusting little brat, Iyaa.

"So what are we going to do about the letter?" Rief asked.

"I don't know," Daclep replied. "Do you think we should do the job?"

"I think so. It would be an awesome adventure!" Iyaa exclaimed.

"Yeah," Somolo agreed.

"We have to think about everyone who will worry about us," Ashin suggested, thinking about how worried his mom was when she didn't know where he was.

"Look, I only have a dad who would worry about me. I've totally got the most carefree type of parent a kid could ever want!" Iyaa bragged.

"We could write notes saying we're on a job and will be back as soon as possible. You never know, we might get money for finding the jewels."

"You never know," Darclep thought aloud. "Or, we might not make it out alive."

"Darclep, you worry too much!" Rief joked.

Inside everybody's mind, they thought about what Darclep just said.

~~~~~~

"I need to look in the forests for the jewel or in the mountains," Yeks grumbled to himself. He levitated above the icy clouds, down into the little Dovevven forest for a closer look. He rubbed his neck, thinking about what his master said. "Master" wasn't his real name. His real name froze your spine whenever it was spoken aloud, alerted all ears when heard: *The Annihilator*... the dark spirit and all evil there ever is, was, and will be.

Yeks and Veil worked for the Annihilator. They were more like slaves than workers, mere mortals paid good money and the power of the dark minds and dark arts. They were there just to do his easy work. When it wasn't done, he didn't fire you, he killed you, along with all of the other people who didn't believe in the Creator, who were enslaved to him, even in death.

Whenever Yeks thought about his dead body being food for the sharks, it made him work even faster! Sweat drenched his garment. He went to the Ceoxdra River to wash the dull stone. Yeks put it in the shining light and noticed it was a topaz. A murky dirty color coated the topaz's true beauty, but for a reason.

"What is so special about these crazy old stones anyway?" he said. "They're worthless!"

~~~~~~

That night, while everyone else in the big house were asleep, Ashin grabbed a cloth bag and stuffed a gourd of water, a loaf of bread, a hunk of cheese, and some venison from that night's dinner into it. He turned to the door of the room where his mom was sleeping. Guilt clouded his mind. It was like not letting the sun shine, but Ashin decided to keep going.

Technically, Ashin wasn't going inside the Nyen forest. He was just standing where it begins.

"Ashin, is that you?"

"Yes."

The dim moonlight revealed a person with wings – Darclep. Standing beside him was a pair of eyes with no visible pupil. Ashin knew who that was! Rief and Somolo rode up on beautiful speckled stallions. The horses' hair waved "hello" in the wind.

"Let's start now," the UBJP leader commanded.

Darclep flew Somolo to the northern part of Xarynthia. Darclep's wings started to ache from the long journey, but he knew he had to go on. He flew back to the southern part of Xarynthia and did the same for the others. Having done his part, the sun shone boldly and it was high in the sky. They began to search. Ashin got a fleeting glimpse of Sacrejhon. Many flashbacks flickered through his memory with just that one look at the golden mountain. He shook the thoughts out of his mind.

"Tip, tap. Tip, tap." Everyone looked around, alerted, fists ready. The sound died away and everyone got back to business. "Tip, tap. Tip, tap." There it was again.

"Agh!" A yell of pain came from Rief's mouth.

Everyone turned around to look at the most sickening thing they'd ever seen. A huge black spider was biting Rief. Darclep electrocuted the spider and it fell down. Rief began to look pale. He gasped for air, violently jerking his body as if that was going to help him get some oxygen.

"Rief, calm down!" said Ashin, concerned about his friend.

"Don't worry, the spider's dead," Darclep announced after examining the fried arachnid.
At that very moment, the spider got up, obviously alive again!

Iyaa scrambled to get Rief out of the way. Somolo grabbed his bow and arrow and shot the spider, but the arrow only grazed its abdomen. The spider charged after Somolo. Ashin made fire come out of his hands, aimed at the spider's feet, but the fire from hands became lighter and lighter until there was none at all. *Oh no!* Ashin thought. *I ran out!*

The spider quickly revived and came after Ashin. He climbed the nearest tree and the spider went after him as far as he could reach. The spider was about to tear him apart, when it slumped and slid off the tree. Ashin saw the hole through the spider's head caused by an arrow. Ashin gave Somolo a grateful smile.

"Thanks!"

Somolo shrugged. "No problem."

As Darclep examined the spider's carcass and crushed it into tiny pieces, he noticed a blood red stone that would not break. He picked it up. "This might be one! What do you think, Somolo?"

"I don't know," said Somolo. There was a confused look on his face. "It seems like it was in the spider. You see no sign of a heart or anything. The jewel must've been his life force!"

"Who knows and who cares? That stone is so dull and ugly. Why would anyone want something so disgusting?" Iyaa's hands were on her hips.

"Iyaa," Ashin sounded irate. "Do you ever have anything good to say?"

"If I did, why would I say it to you?"

"Please stop, both of you!" Darclep shouted. "It makes no sense to keep this stone, but at the same time, just in case, maybe it does. We'll vote. Who thinks we should keep this stone?" Darclep and Ashin's hands shot up.

"Who thinks we *shouldn't* keep the stone?" Somolo and Iyaa's hands shot up. Everyone turned to Rief. He squirmed to get his hand up as much as possible. Darclep threw the stone in disappointment.

"Okay then, let's go," commanded Somolo. Ashin stayed a few steps behind. He grabbed the stone before anybody saw him.

As the sun started to set, they tried to keep Rief alive. Except for their clothes or food sack, there was no cloth to wrap his bite wound and nobody was willing to donate any of that.

"It's not that bad," Rief said as confidently as possible, trying to make the others feel better, but he wondered how long he'd live with the spider's poison in his body. *Why did I leave home?* he asked himself. *I won't live to get back there.*

Everybody ate very little to ration their food. They didn't know how long they'd be on this odyssey! Iyaa made a fire and everybody gathered around like it was a god. Somolo rubbed his hand above the flames. Ashin put his hands in the fire to get more heat energy. Iyaa put on a sweet smile, but Ashin saw her eyes dancing with happiness because he'd run out of fuel.

"So Darclep, how did you end up in Soclid?" Iyaa asked curiously.

"Well," he began, "my mom wanted to move to Baltham, where she's from, but my dad is from Faristana, so he wanted to move there. We ended up here, halfway between, as a compromise and resolve the argument."

"What about you, Somolo?"

"I don't want to talk about it!" he grunted.

"Rief?"

"My mom died and my dad is from Soclid, so we moved here."

"What about you, Ashin?" she asked in a cheery voice. Iyaa smiled that sweet smile and raised her eyebrows. Ashin glared at her for what seemed like the thousandth time and paused before he answered. *I'll bet she's testing me, to see if I let my anger get the best of me. I'll show her!*

"We decided to move here with Doshan," Ashin said calmly. *Actually, why did we move to Soclid?* Ashin wondered.

The hypnotizing chirping of crickets led all of the kids to their cots for a slumber.

~~~~~~

The next morning, the children traveled off the roads so as not to raise suspicion. Rief's glassy eyes stared into space. He was strapped onto a stallion because he was unable to walk. A tear slowly rolled down of his cheek.

"Stop!" Ashin warned. Everybody looked at him strangely. "This is Wea Woods, also know as Double W," he said. "These are natural born gallows!"

"Sure," Iyaa replied sarcastically and set off running.

Darclep rolled his eyes. "I'll go after her."

Iyaa zigzagged through Double W moving at angular turns as the trees tried to grab her. She wasn't paying attention to where she was going and a tree grabbed her off her horse.

"Why are you in my kingdom?" A booming voice seem to come from the tree. The tree's grip around her neck became tight. Her head felt like it would explode and there was no way to stop the pain. She gasped for air…

~~~~~~

Darclep ran through the same woods, constantly looking back to see if Rief was still on the horse. A tree's long arms grabbed for Darclep, but he made a quick turn the opposite way. He did that over and over as different trees tried to grab him. He turned back to see if Rief was still behind him, he wasn't there. Darclep started to panic.

"Where is he?"Darclep wondered out loud.

"Right here!" A voice said. The tree wrung Rief's neck, then dropped him on the ground.

"Noooo!" Darclep wailed. "I have to get out of here!"

Darclep closed his eyes to get the image of his friend's pale blue face out of his mind. He clutched his stomach and kicked the horse into a gallop.

~~~~~~

Ashin waited and waited, but no one came. He finally saw Darclep up in the sky. A force led by Darclep's hand was around his horse, which was also in the air.

"Did you find her?" Somolo asked when Darclep and his horse landed.

"No," Darclep replied. "Ashin, go find her."

Ashin groaned. "Why not Somolo?"

"Just go!" Frustration was apparent in Darclep's voice. "What's wrong with you? You know these woods better than we do."

Reluctantly, Ashin mounted the horse and rode off to find Iyaa. He looked around cautiously. He was about to give up and leave the brat to die when he heard a slight whisper.

"Ashin, help me." The girl was barely able to get the words out of her mouth. Ashin circled around a few times until he finally found her.

"Ahhh!" screamed the tree, but only for a moment before Ashin burned it down to molecule-sized ashes.

Iyaa fell to the ground, trying to collect her breath. "Thanks."

"You need to learn to listen!" Ashin scolded. "I'm sick of hearing that smart-aleck tone in your voice saying 'It's Iyaa's way every day!'"

At first, Iyaa looked shocked, but then she recovered. "By who, you? I was never taught to listen. So tell me, do you have any other bright ideas?"

Ashin and Iyaa rode the horse ran out of Wea Woods. They saw Somolo's and Darclep's melancholy faces. "What's wrong?" Ashin asked.

Somolo looked up. "Rief died."

"I saw it all," Darclep's voice was trembling. "After the tree wrung his neck, he fell to the ground. The Snakes for the Dead appeared and chained him to the ground and a tan-colored cobra bit him in the middle of his forehead." Darclep shuddered. It felt like somebody had rubbed snow all over his bare back.

"From the top of Rief's head to the bottom of his feet, he became transparent. The snakes led him to the core of our world, Doclazhec, where the dead swim. The core is right below Htevaon, the dark and evil mountain. In other words, he didn't make it," said Ashin. He didn't feel sorry for Rief because he hadn't known him for a long time, but there was a little bit of sadness because he knew the boy when he was alive.

They camped a few miles away from Wea Woods. No one touched the food and hardly a word was spoken. Ashin sat up and thought about everything that had happened that day. *Why didn't I just say 'you're welcome' when Iyaa thanked me?* Ashin wondered. *Why do I always have to try to prove my point? Why can't I just keep my mouth shut for once?*

Leaves rustled a few yards away. An alert Ashin turned to scan the open area. He crept toward the sound and peered through the bushes. There in the moonlight sat Iyaa, making fuel for herself, getting ready for the next day.

"I'm sorry," she said, then paused, "Ashin."

Hearing her say his name startled him. "How did you know I was here?"

"I can read minds," she said without turning around. "All Wabhycs can read minds... even biracial ones." Iyaa's shoulders slumped like a sunflower at nighttime.

"I'm the one who should be saying I'm sor---"

"No!" Iyaa cut him off. "I confess, it's true. I do need to learn how to listen, but some things you need each part of a family for and I don't have that. It's the same for

60

you -- you totally need your dad to slap you around sometime." Her tone was dead serious. Iyaa avoided looking at him, staring absentmindedly into the starry sky. "Sometimes both parents need to be there to teach you. One can't do it alone."

Ashin nodded, then turned to leave. He needed to get some sleep. Before he drifted off, he thought hard about what she'd said. *So much for my apology, but I guess she forgave me.*

5

Veil cut through Karcickel Valley to the border of Baltham. Her face glistened in the sunlight from the sweat trickling down and lay upon her clothing.

A bald-headed man had his backside facing Karcickel Valley. Through the corner of his eye, he saw Veil coming up the path. A black hooded cloak covered her face so that only her mysterious eyes were visible. He handed her a wad of paper. She handed him a pouch. It jingled when he moved it. Veil looked at the paper, smiled, then threw it on the ground. When she left, the man opened the pouch and grabbed a handful of copper coins out of the bag. His thin lips split into a wide smile as the coins ran through his fingers. He put them back in the pouch and headed back to Baltham.

~~~~~~

When the sun rose the next day, everybody ate some of venison that Somolo had hunted and killed. When they were ready to depart, Darclep used his Balthamian powers to pick up Ashin. They flew tandem while Iyaa and Somolo rode the stallions. This time, Ashin led the way.

The horses trotted to the edge of the Dovevven Forest where the riders had to stop. Somolo and Iyaa tied the horses to a tree as Darclep and Ashin floated down to the moist green grass.

"Wow!" said Somolo, dazzled by the beauty of the Dovevven Forest, its carpet of grass and daffodils on the forest's floor and its majestic scenery that could only be seen from a bird's eye view high in the sky. The branches looked like they were waving hello, saying "Look at me! Don't you just love my hair?" Some of the trees looked like they wore jewelry, earrings made of the fruit they bore.

Somolo stepped back to get a better point of view, when he felt something poke him.
"Ouch!" he said, startled, but calmed down when he saw an old man about his own size. He had long white hair and a matching beard.

The man was fuming mad. His face was turning redder by the second! "Are you blind, eh?" the elder sparked.

"No," Somolo mumbled.

"Then watch where you're going!"

Somolo shrugged. "Sorry." Somolo walked back to where the UBJP members were looking at something. The elder watched them closely.

"Is this one?" Iyaa asked, picking up a small, delicate-looking purple stone.

"No, it has to be shiny and one on this list."

The elder cleared his throat and all the children turned around. He put his shovel on the ground. "You're looking for the only jewels in all of Doclazhec, too, eh?" he asked.

"Yes…" Ashin said slowly, allowing his answer to trail off. The old man looked familiar, as if he'd seen him a few years ago.

"My name is Yeks. I already found one of the jewels." He pulled the dull-coated topaz from his pocket. "First of all, all of the jewels are dull and dirty, not shiny."

The kids looked at him confused. "Why?" Darclep asked.

"Oh, you don't know the story? Well, I'll tell you. The jewels represent the unclean hearts of the favored before they know the Creator."

Ashin remembered the name Yeks. It was from a rhyme that schoolchildren used to sing a year after the Summer Flood.

> *Yek's hex*
> *The weather he checks*
> *When it's good, he makes it bad*
> *So stay inside to be a good lad*

Maybe there are many people with the name Yeks, Ashin wondered. *But there are hardly any people who look like and might be the real Yeks.*

"Oh, no!" Darclep howled. "How could I be so stupid?"

"What?" Somolo said.

"We didn't get the other stone! You know, the one from the spider? We threw it away!"

Everyone groaned.

"No, we didn't." said Ashin "I kept it." He pulled it out of his pouch and the kids sighed in relief.

"We owe it to you, Ashin." Somolo said. Ashin's smile grew wide. Yeks again cleared his throat to get their attention. Ashin stepped back, thinking about how they would have had only one, not two of the seven jewels. They'd have to be really careful around him.

"You could help me find them and I can help all of you," Yeks suggested. "Deal?"

"Deal," Somolo agreed. Yeks and Somolo shook hands. Yeks smiled slyly. For the first time that day, his hair seemed to be alive! His head and neck were no longer going to be on a platter, at least for now.

~~~~~~

Meanwhile, Veil looked into her crystal ball. "Wohsem ylno Yekka!" she whispered.

Then Yeks appeared in the crystal ball. *Veil, can you hear me?* he telepathed.

"Yes."

Well, I've got some 'helpers' with me, so I should be done in no time. Now we have three, so we only need to find four. Great, eh?

"Yes, very. Now get back to work!"

The conversation was a brief one. Business was business, but not even Veil knew why she was doing what she was doing. All she knew was to follow the Master's orders and be done with it... or else.

~~~~~~

In one day, they looked all over Dovevven Forest to find the jewels. Everyone split up to dig holes, then refilled them, having found nothing. Despondency was felt by the whole group.

I'm ready to go home, Ashin thought, but set that thought aside because he had to finish this task, at least he felt he had to anyway.

The next day, Darclep flew Iyaa to Baltham and waited for Yeks, Ashin, and Somolo. The village they landed in was Kooblec. It was an extremely busy place. Hundreds of people were heard talking at the same time... selling meat or produce, counting to be sure they'd been paid. People overflowed the village. Kids played in the streets. Horses trotted or galloped in many different directions, frequently making it difficult for pedestrians to either get on or get off the streets. It wouldn't surprise anyone to learn that anyone who'd lived in this village for any length of time ran the risk of being trampled. It was said that as many as thirty people had gotten trampled in a single day.

Darclep's mouth dropped open at the sight of this place. His eyes widened in wonder and amazement. Iyaa folded her arms. Her deep brown tunic stood still. It had no sleeves and was only an inch below her knees. Iyaa had put on some pants under the tunic because she was going on a trip, something her father would never have allowed.

"Iyaa!" her father would yell.

"Yes, Papa?" she would politely answer, as if nothing was going on.

"Why are you wearing your cousin Tyl's pants?"

"I want to play some rough games with him, like wrestling, and you have to have pants on for those games, right, Papa?"

"Take them off immediately!"

"Yes, Papa." Iyaa would walk away with that mischievous sparkle in her eye. She wished she and her dad would move to Wabhyc so she could have some girls as strong as her to fight with. Iyaa's senses were quickly aroused, bringing her back to reality when she saw Yeks, Somolo, and Ashin.

Keep going south of that bustling village. I have a friend waiting to see you. Keep going until it gets quiet, then go to the first farm you see, Veil telepathed.

Okay, Yeks replied. "Follow me," he told the kids. "I have a friend who lives outside of this settlement."

The deafening sounds of the village died down as they came towards flat lands that were barren except for the green grass that seemed to be painted over the surface of the dirt.

The sun had started to set. Yeks nervously twisted a lock of his hair. *Where is that rotten farm? Had Veil lied to him? She wouldn't,* he decided. *Not when there's business to be done!* Yeks' temper was reaching the boiling point! It had to be here.

"Hello," said a deep voice. If a lion could talk, that's how it would sound. The kids and Yeks were frightened. Their hearts were beating faster than ever! Standing right behind them was a man with eyes the size of tennis balls, thick eyebrows which connected above his wide, flat nose, and paper-thin lips. He had no hair. In other words, he was totally bald.

"My name is Pepli," said the man. "And you are...?"

"My name is Yeks and this is--"

"Oh, then I am delighted to see you for this special appointment, my friend," Pepli interrupted, emphasizing the words "special" and "appointment." He turned to the kids. "Are these your children?"

"No!" replied Yeks, feeling quite abashed. His checks reddened. "These are some kids I met in the Dovevven Forest. They were also looking for the only jewels in Doclazhec!"

Pepli showed no interest in the subject of the jewels. He didn't make a move. His lips formed a straight line across his face. "Let me show you to my home," he said at last, then turned and led the way.

Ashin thought Pepli was acting very peculiar towards Yeks. *They definitely weren't friends, maybe acquaintances, but nothing more.*

It was nighttime when the group made it to Pepli's house, but it was worth the walk! They had a feast of pork seasoned with herbs from the Omni Mountains. The Omni Mountains were the third largest of all the mountains, Sacrejhon being the first largest and Htevaon the second. They also enjoyed a huge loaf of bread, grape juice, apples, and honey. They dined alone as Pepli, his son, and his wife Yonna, had eaten earlier that day and were sound asleep in their beds.

After everybody ate, they laid on their cots in an old, hideous-looking barn.

"Darclep?" Ashin called out.

"Yes?"

"When did you get your wings?"

Darclep turned to face Ashin. "I was an early bird. I got them when I was seven. Most Fairies and Fardons get them when they're around nine to eleven. They're little at first, the size of your hands, then in about a month, maybe less, they grow to their full size."

No response came from Ashin. "You're thinking about Doshan, huh?" Darclep asked quietly. He saw it all over Ashin's face.

"Yeah."

"I'm sorry, but we can't re-do it. We're on a mission, remember? We're not in Soclid!"Darclep turned over and curled up, trying to get warm. "Now go to sleep."

Those words were useless. Darclep didn't have to waste his breath because Ashin stayed awake most of the night. He heard some dampening noises outside of the barn and scrambled close to the barn's doors.

"We need to dig in your land... just to check... just in case." Yeks' voice was easy to recognize.

"No! She gave me strict instructions about dealing with you... and that's one of them I'm not allowed to do," Pepli's dry voice rumbled deeply.

"Then why bring me here? Does she want me to find them?" asked Yeks.

"I don't know."

Ashin returned to his cot. He lay awake most of the night until he could no longer hold them open anymore.

After a breakfast of eggs and lightly toasted bread, spread with scrumptious apple butter, the kids went outside to play a game suggested by Iyaa -- wrestling. If course, Iyaa beat everybody. Darclep was tricky, but easy. She used fire to drain his power, then popped him in the head a few times.

Pepli's son walked up to watch the games. He looked a lot like his father except for his black hair, white eyes, and his chubby build. "Hello," he said to get everyone's attention. "My name is Anar."

"Hey!" they chorused.

"I know you are not brothers and sister, so what are you?"

"We're members of the UBJP," Iyaa blurted out. "It stands for Underground Biracial Juveniles with Powers." The boys glared at her.

"We forgot to tell her that it is supposed to be kept secret!" Darclep gave an agitated whisper to Ashin.

"Sorry," said Iyaa, noticing the glares.

"Well," Anar began. "I challenge all of you UBJP members to a wrestling match."

"I'll go first," said Somolo, standing up. "But first, how old are you?"

"Thirteen," said Anar.

"Wow, you're the same age as me!" Somolo nodded contently.

The fight was on. It happened too fast in Ashin's opinion. Anar walked through Somolo's Balthamian without feeling a thing. As he moved towards Somolo, Anar's completely white eyes stared directly at Somolo and in that instant, Somolo knew he was going to lose.

"I might as well say right now, I'm a normal person," Somolo said, skulking away from Anar, who was getting ready to punch him for the second time.

"Aren't you the captain of the UBJP?" Anar asked.

"Yes," Somolo replied.

Anar rolled his eyes. "I'm sure everyone in this crew can fight better than you with the puny little power you have!"

Somolo gasped in shock. That hurt. He wasn't expecting that. He stopped in his tracks, then immediately felt a huge blow to the back of his head. He watched himself go down. He felt helpless, like there was nothing he could do. His heart cried.

After a few more punches, Anar called out, "Who's next?"

Darclep huddled with Ashin and Iyaa. "Don't do this, especially you, Ashin. You'll have broken ribs in seconds!"

"Why aren't you giving Iyaa any reason why she should do it?" Ashin was fuming.

Darclep looked him straight in the eye. "Because she's stronger than you are." Ashin couldn't argue with that.

"I'll show Anar!" Iyaa said, storming to the middle of the grass where Anar waited.
Anar tried hard not to laugh as she walked towards him. He bent over to kiss her hand and she swung her fist toward his jaw. *Oh no you don't!* she thought.

Anar caught her other arm and swung her into a tree. She slid down. "You really think I would, huh?" Anar snarled. "I have eyes, you know!" As he came closer, Iyaa tripped him. He fell on his bottom and smirked. "Seriously, you don't fight like a real Wabhyc."

Both of them traded punches back and forth. They weren't wrestling anymore. Tears were running down Iyaa cheeks, but they were hardly visible. She tripped him again. Anar looked annoyed. Iyaa couldn't stand it when kids, especially boys, acted like that because she was a girl. She jumped on his legs.

"Ahhh!" Anar screamed in agony.

She kicked at his ribs, then grabbed his hand and burned him. Instantly, the fire swallowed him. He screamed in pain. Ashin grabbed Iyaa's hand and pulled her away from the fight. Darclep went with them. She sat down, pulled her knees up to her head, and sniveled.

"Fighting when you're mad actually makes you weaker," Darclep told her.

Iyaa balled up her fist. "When I get my hands on him, I'm going to kill him."

Ashin grinned. "Works for me!"

"You're not helping," Darclep hissed at Ashin. "Say that again and you both can just forget this trip and finding the jewels!" Darclep turned to Iyaa. "You're letting his mocking get the best of you. Trust me, it's his strength. He's not strong."

Iyaa continued to cry, letting her anger out with every drop of salty liquid coming out of her eyes. Ashin and Darclep left her to cry off the rest of the day.

The sun rose like every other morning. The kids woke up in time to see the beautiful sunrise as they breathed in the fresh scents of nature.

"I don't think Pepli and his family would mind if we dig, so let's get to work," Somolo commanded.

Ashin, Darclep, Iyaa, and Somolo grabbed some shovels and started digging. Sweat began to pour down their faces as the sun was fully risen. Yeks came outside and started working too. Pepli looked outside to see what was causing all the racket. What he saw caused his eyes to widened. His nose flared out and his eyebrows narrowed. Pepli ran out of his house, furious about what they were doing.

"What did I tell you about digging in my land for that crazy jewel? Stop right now!" He yelled. "Yonna, Anar, get them!" A chubby woman with short black hair ran outside. Anar was already there.

Ashin turned and ran with all of his might, but he tripped over a rock and fell. "Guys, help me!" Ashin he cried, but no one came. Everybody just kept running. It was like déjà vu to Ashin. He couldn't believe that the dream he had was basically coming true!"

Yonna and Pepli grabbed hold of Ashin and dragged him inside of the house while Anar continued to chase the others. Ashin felt a burn from the carpet, then splinters as his body was dragged through the house, then downstairs into a basement.

"Nane, Doflop, meet your new roommate!" said Pepli as Ashin was thrown into the room and Yonna locked door.

~~~~~~

"Veil is going to be so angry with me. When she finds out, the first thing she's going to do is kill me!" Horror filled Pepli's mind. "She wanted all of Yeks' helpers captured, not just one!"

"There, there," Yonna tried to soothe her fidgety husband. "It's going to be all right." But she was thinking the same thing. They needed the money Veil had given to Pepli!

~~~~~~

Anar ran trying to catch up with the others. He pulled out his bow and arrow. His target was Iyaa. The arrow flew off the old bow and grazed Iyaa's arm. The wind had changed, causing the arrow to go off course and into the center of Somolo's heart.

Why couldn't I have died? Darclep thought, seeing the whole thing. *Why did it have to be my best friend?*

Darclep pushed Iyaa forward. "Go on with Yeks." His voice sounded hoarse, like a frog's as he choaked out the words. Tears ran down his cheeks. *Why? Why Somolo?*

"Isn't that a beauty?" a voice said.

"Anar." Darclep's voice was full of hate. "Murderer! I'll show you death!" Darclep yelled as he punched Anar in the jaw. Darclep picked Anar up and flew him high into the air, over the trees, higher and higher into clouds until the village, the houses, even the waters looked diminutive. "I hope you know how to swim," he said before he dropped Anar into the middle of Voel Lake.

Anar's arms flailed wildly as he fell. Moments after he hit the water, his head appeared above the water's surface, gasping for air. Darclep loved the sight, enjoying the sight of Anar's last moments of life. Darclep felt blame hover above him. *I'm just doing this as payback. It's revenge to watch him die!*

Let the boy out! Another piece of his mind was telling him something he didn't want to hear. Darclep remained still for a few minutes, then although still fuming, he swooped down and plucked Anar from the waves.

"Thanks," said Anar, coughing up water.

"Just go home and leave the rest of us alone! I should've gone ahead and killed you!"

"Look, I'm seriously sorry. I know it was wrong, but I wasn't trying to kill him." Anar knew better than to say 'Can you please forgive me?' because he knew that 'No!' would have been the answer.

77

"It's wrong either way -- killing the other person wouldn't make it right!" Darclep scolded. "Besides, who were you trying to kill?"

"I think you know."

Darclep dropped Anar off, but he forgot to pick up one person: Ashin.

~~~~~~

Ashin crawled into the corner of the basement, feeling his way because it was too dark to see. His stomach roared inside of him. "I left home for this?" he wondered aloud.

"It's what why we all left home." Ashin heard a male voice say.

He turned his hand into fire and carefully moved it around to see who else was there. Sitting next to the side wall to his right was a male Xarynthian. His hair looked black because there wasn't enough light. Ashin thought about setting the place on fire, but that would kill these people too, so he banished the thought. Sitting near the wall opposite the Xarynthian was a Fairy, a female Faristanian. Her wings had been clipped off.

"What's your name?" the man asked.

"Ashin."

The man's eyes widened with shock. "Is it you? Is it really you?"

"Uh…" Ashin was baffled. The look on the man's face made him feel uneasy.

"I'm sorry," the Xarynthian said, clearing his throat. "Are you Sade's only son?"

"How do you know my father?"

"I'm his brother, Doflon."

"How did you end up here?"

"The same way you did, but it's a much more complicated story."

"Who is she?" Ashin asked, pointing to the Fairy who sat there knitting. She looked sixteen, but Ashin didn't dare ask how old she really was.

"That's Nane. She came here about two years ago."

Sadness made Nane's skin wrinkled and bones frail. *I'm sure my family thinks I'm dead!* she thought. "Are you hungry?" she asked Ashin.

"Yes, very!" Ashin eagerly replied. He was ravenous!

Nane sprinkled fairy dust on his hands and suddenly food appeared! Ashin quickly gobbled it down.

"Thanks." Ashin replied, very grateful for what she'd done.

"You're welcome."

Ashin felt tired and soon fell asleep.

~~~~~~

Veil narrowed her eyes.

"That fool!" she shouted. She pounded on the table. It cracked and shattered. "I asked for all of the kids and he only gave me one!"

She pounded on the rock wall with her hand. Pebbles, boulders, and other debris fell down and caved in the room she occupied.

~~~~~~

Yeks stopped running. He bent over, panting, as sweat poured down his face. Iyaa did the same.

Veil, are you there?

Yeks, what do you think?

That guy was trying to capture me!

I know. It was supposed to look like you were with the group so we could lead them there.

Okay.

After Yeks stopped telepathing, he noticed Iyaa was in a peculiar posture. The forefinger and middle finger of each of her hands were pressed against each of her temples. After a while, she opened her eyes.

"A jewel is in the Ceoxdra River. I don't know where, but it is!"

"You used your wishes, eh?"

"Just one."

Darclep landed on the earthen path they were following.

"Darclep, fly me to the headwaters of the Ceoxdra River."

~~~~~~

Ashin woke up to the noise of birds. He was about to get up when he remembered he was in Pepli's wretched basement. He squeezed his eyes closed, then opened them again as if that would make the nightmare go away.

"Wake up, lad," said Doflon. "You've got to eat. Nane didn't feel like making any food today."

"That is just selfish!" Ashin grumbled.

"Pepli would just use Nane, Ashin…if they knew she had fairy dust." Doflon explained.

Ashin grabbed a piece of stale bread, crunched, and tried to chew on it. The bread tasted like roaches with flour over them. The after-taste was worse. It was like a rotten food you love that you ate anyway. Ashin held his throat trying to get the taste out of his mouth.

Ashin's mind was not on food. He wanted to get out of there and started feeling around the basement's low ceiling. "Is there any opening to this basement besides the door?" Ashin asked.

"Yes," Nane replied, "but you would never make it out alive."

"Why not?"

"Jilla and Tem." Nane replied. "Jilla is the night owl who guards this basement at night to make sure we don't get out. If we do, she'll tear us to pieces. We saw it happen once. Tem is the day hawk who watches his prey, just like Jilla."

"Oh." Ashin's face fell upon hearing the disappointing news. *I'm going to die in here!*

He changed the subject. "Do fairies have at least one major power?"

At first Nane looked offended, but then her face resumed its serene demeanor. "Yes… kindness." That wasn't the answer Ashin was looking for. He was hoping she'd say something else. "Do you have a Fairy or a Fardon friend?" Nane asked.

"Yes, a biracial Fardon, though. His name is Doshan."

Nane took the fairy dust she was holding and threw it out of the opening on the roof before the day hawk Tem could bite her hand off. She witnessed the wind stop to picking up her dust, then keep going. "I hope you don't mind, but I just sent a message to Doshan. Hopefully he'll get it."

Iyaa dipped her feet into the ice-cold Ceoxdra River, then quickly pulled them out. She shivered with fear. Winter was coming and if the ice dominated the heat in her body, which is more than a normal human's, she would die. She turned to Yeks and Darclep.

"Look," she said. "I have a better chance of surviving this if the snow doesn't come yet. Let me find this one."

"Okay," Darclep reluctantly agreed. "Just let me know. This trip can take from three weeks to three months."

"What if we look for the rest of the jewels while she's on this journey?" Yeks suggested.

"Well," Darclep hesitated. *What if she dies in the cold? She's very independent and she doesn't listen, so she'd still do it, even if I told her no.* "Okay," he finally said with a sigh. "Good luck."

"Good luck to you, too," said Iyaa, hugging him tightly.

"Easy!" Darclep stiffened up at first, but then he relaxed, patting her back. She reminded him of his younger sister, Sala. It took pain for Sala to stop doing dangerous things. "Telepath us every night."

"Okay." And with that she dove into the river.

7

A boy with deep brown hair and wings left his school when the giant bell rang loudly, the sound vibrating in his ears. When dust fell to the ground out of nowhere, he scooped it up.

"Doshan, help us!" it said.

Doshan knew who it was. The wind picked up the dust again. Doshan flew and followed it. His white wings inhaled and exhaled the sunlight's soft rays. The day after he was kicked out of the UBJP, he found he had wings. They were very tiny, hardly visible. The day after that, they got sturdier. His family noticed them immediately. "You finally have your wings!" they said. Now he could try them out. It only took them a week to grow to their adult size because they grew rapidly. It took him another week to get used to flying and bearing extra weight, but he made it!

Doshan went to his house to leave his mother and father a note, then went on his way. Doshan took out some dust and covered himself with it. He was enjoying the view when he came to Baltham, a place he'd never been before. The flat fields were dressed in a rainbow of flowers. In the distance he saw the Omni Mountains painted with snow. The river's water leapt over nearby boulders. The dust finally settled on the roof of an old dingy-looking house.

"Caw! Caw!" a hawk cried out. It was looking directly at Doshan and flew towards him. As it swooped down, it turned into a human man. His curly hair was wild, looking like it hadn't been groomed in years. His tunic was tattered.

Doshan and the man tumbled to the ground, punching each other. Tem turned his hands into hawk's claws and dug them into Doshan's shoulders. Doshan screamed in pain. The man got up and Doshan kicked him in the stomach. The man fell down, but then got up again. His eyebrows furrowed like lightning cutting through dark clouds. He picked up Doshan and threw him. Doshan landed on his backside.

"Ow!" Doshan groaned. "Stay conscious." He was getting weary and the sun was going down. The man ran towards him. Suddenly Tem's wings grew onto his human form and so did a beak! He tore part one of Doshan's wings.

"Jilla!" shouted Tem.

"Yes, Tem?" Doshan heard a female voice respond. An owl landed on the ground and transformed into a woman. As she came into Doshan's sight, he saw she was as burly as Tem! Jilla saw the intruder and flew towards him at warp speed.
"Hello, young boy," she said. "Leave now before you get hurt!"

Doshan stood up, shaking his head. Tem turned into a bird and went back to fighting Doshan. He sunk his claws into Doshan's stomach. Doshan clenched his teeth and his eyes began to water. He could taste blood in the back of his throat. Jilla tore at his wings, ripping them more, until Doshan cried out.

"We are birds of prey. You should have listened to your studies. We will tear your flesh apart."

Doshan touched Jilla's and Tem's throats, baked their insides with lightning. He used fairy dust like a salve and all of his wounds instantly disappeared! Doshan flew up to the roof and dived inside the opening.

"Doshan, is that you?" asked Ashin.

"Yes, Ashin."

"I hardly recognized you!"

"Yeah. Well, let's get goin--"

"Wait!" said Nane. She pulled a green murky stone out of her pocket and handed it to Ashin. "I found this before I was captured. I want you to have it."

Ashin smiled. "Thank you."

Ashin, Doshan, Doflon, and Nane quietly crept out of the basement. Once outside, they said goodbye and went their separate ways. Even though it was nighttime, Ashin's heart felt free, as if it could pop out of his body, spread wings and fly!

It was very quiet as Ashin and Doshan walked along a path. "Doshan," Ashin said to break the silence. "I'm sorry for the way I acted. I should have said I'm not going to be in it either. I guess I was blinded by my pride. You don't have to forgive, but I played my part in reconciliation. I learned a lot during this journey and I know I will be a different boy from now on, one that those who know me have never seen before."

"Well, you will be a different person because in the eyes of your family, including your mom's, Ashin is dead!"

Ashin gasped with horror as Doshan turned to face him. "Your gravestone is right outside your house. If you don't have any more pride like you said, you'd go back home and stop thinking that nobody's worried about you!" Doshan stopped talking to let Ashin think a little bit, then added, "Or was!"

Ashin looked at Doshan who stared straight ahead. Ashin knew who he was talking about. For the first time in Ashin's life, somebody told him straight up that his biggest weakness was his pride.

~~~~~~

The next morning, Veil levitated the diamond impure stone. It transformed into an irregular shape and she nearly dropped it! She rotated it in her hand, gazing at it warily until she was satisfied, then she put it down.

Veil telepathed Pepli. *Meet me at the border of Baltham.*

~~~~~~

Pepli shivered. He knew *she* knew. When he saw there was no one in the basement and his two guards, Jilla and Tem, had disappeared, the color disappeared from his face. He practically fainted.

Pepli kept walking towards the border. He gulped when he saw Veil there waiting for him. She had what looked like a huge bag of coppers with her.

"Hello, Pepli," she said flatly. "You did so well that I'm giving you this right now." Veil hit him in the back of his head with the huge bag of rocks. Pepli was so stunned and fell to the ground. "I asked for all of those 'helpers' of Yek's to be snared and put in a cage, but you gave me none of them!" Veil screamed.

She pulled out a dagger. Pepli tried to get up, but her sorcery magic trapped him on the ground. She knelt beside him. "Just like you gave me none of them, in this world there will be none of you!" Veil raised the dagger above her head, then plunged it into Pepli's heart, knowing he would live just long enough to feel the pain of his own death. "I'll tell your family you said goodbye!"

The cobra slipped up from the ground and climbed onto Pepli's forehead. Its bite was on target and some of the poison trickled onto the ground. Veil watched in delight. A smirk crept onto her face like a black widow spider watching an insect caught in its web. As Pepli became transparent, Veil noticed a contaminated jewel in his heart. She reached down and picked it up.
"Oh, how pretty! Quartz!"

Iyaa poked her head out of the water to get some air and quickly scouted the area before the fierce waters pulled her back down. She moved on, swimming deeper into the river's sparkling water. *Where is that crazy stone?* she wondered.

Suddenly a huge fish appeared out of nowhere. It was a depressing cloudy gray with needles, knives, and daggers as teeth. "Mmm…something smells good." The fish breathed in the scent through his acute gills. "Is it flounder? No, no, I smell catfish. No, I'm so foolish, it's Wabhycian flesh!" The fish snapped at Iyaa and she hurried to the surface. She wasn't a fast swimmer and the fish bit her ankle. Iyaa let out a piercing scream, which would have been much louder if she were on land. Iyaa tried to wrestle her foot from the fish's grip, but it held on.

I'm going to give it to you and that's all I got!

Iyaa kicked the fish's head with her other foot. It loosed its grip on her ankle and she kept swimming as fast as she could, leaving a trail of blood behind her. When she finally reached the riverbank, she looked at her injury. Skin had been scraped off her ankle and there was a huge bite mark through her flesh, all the way to the bone, but she hadn't lost her foot. Iyaa ripped off part of her pant leg and tied it around her sore, bleeding ankle.

Having escaped the fish, she realized that she was hungry. She was annoyed with herself for failing to bringing any weapons to use for hunting food. She didn't want to wish for one, though, because she had to keep track of her wishes and didn't want to waste one. Suddenly, she had an idea. She limped to the water's edge, put out her arms until she saw the shadow of a fish. When it jumped out of the water, she caught it and burned it, then gutted it and peeled off the skin. By the end of the day, she had ten fish killed, gutted, peeled, and ready to eat!

~~~~~~

Darclep was worried. The group had been split up. *Ashin was captured and Iyaa was in the Ceoxdra River. This is just great!*

"Yeks, can you telepath?"

"Yes, why do you ask?"

"Could you telepath Ashin?"

Yeks shook his head no.

Darclep groaned his loudest. "Why not? We need to bring the UBJP kids back together and I need your help!"

Yeks sighed. "Okay, I will." He put his index finger and middle finger to his temple. "He's at the Omni Mountains. Let's go."

Darclep and Yeks flew into the air.

~~~~~~

Veil chuckled when she peered into her crystal ball. She made it levitate back to its original place. She walked into almost every dark room inside of Htevaon. She went into a dungeon. It was unique because it had an invisible shield around each prisoner. She unlocked them all, one at a time, saying to each, "I need your help."
Once the air hit them, they transformed into mud…

Darclep and Yeks flew to the Omni Mountains where they saw a tent and a person with large wings standing in front of it. They floated down to see the face of the person. Yeks looked at the person suspiciously, as he had never met them before.

"Hello, Doshan," Darclep greeted. Doshan nodded in return. Darclep stared at him as if he was trying to figure out what was different about him. Doshan looked older than his age. His bleached white wings made him look proud, courageous, and a bit… like a teenager. He would surely pass. His medium-sized eyes held a frosty glare. His small lips formed a bitter frown.

At that moment, Ashin crawled out of the tent and welcomed them. He hadn't exactly changed, but his shirt was shredded. "Nane, a young lady we met, gave us an emerald. Now we have three out of seven," Ashin informed them.

Darclep yawned. "Look, I'm ready to give up. This is taking too long. We still have more than half of the jewels to find. What's the use of going on?"

Ashin shrugged. "And?"

"Too many have already died -- and we might be next!" Darclep continued. "Are we willing to risk our own lives for some crazy jewels that we don't even know we'll get any money for even if we are able to find them!"

Everything was still. Not even a bird song was heard. Everyone stared at Darclep, but in their minds, they each thought about everything he'd just said.

"Because of this craziness, I'm the only original Underground Biracial Juvenile with Powers left." Darclep could barely get the words out of his mouth. "I know I worry a lot, but it's the truth. All of us might not make this journey."

~~~~~~

After having eaten a great meal the night before, Iyaa was re-energized. She felt like could swim for two more days, but her ankle wasn't feeling too good. She dragged herself over to some trees. Nearby was a hollow log and beside it was a knife. Iyaa shaved off the top of the log, leaving only the bottom half to use as a raft. She loaded her leftover fish and was off. The freezing cold water pummeled her in the face, caking her with soft ice as she glided along in the raft. *I'm not going to stop until the water has crossed Soclid,* she told herself.

Sharp shards of ices jumped out of the water and cut Iyaa's skin open on the same arm the arrow grazed her arm. Iyaa traveled on for some time before she felt cold drops on her face. She looked up and groaned. *It's snowing! That's the last thing I need right about now!* Once the snow started to fall heavier, she was resigned to stopping for the day. She pulled her raft onto the bank as far as she could, then sat down resting her back against it. She became quite drowsy, but forced her eyes open every time she started to drift off. "Stay awake, Iyaa!" she shouted out loud, but it didn't work. She was too tired and soon fell asleep.

The next morning, Iyaa woke up to find herself covered with snow. Panicked, she put her hand on her forehead, then calmed down. *My temperature isn't decreasing, at least for right now.* She nibbled on some fish. "Don't eat too much!" she scolded herself. "I need to save some for later."

She swept the snow off herself and the raft, then set off again. The river swept her and her makeshift craft downstream, raced along as if it was in a big hurry to get somewhere. The Alodot part of the river was like a descending a staircase, moving as swiftly as the wind!

"What is that brushing against my hair?" she wondered, hoping it wasn't another one of those fishes. She turned her head and saw a huge wooden boat going the same direction she was!
Oh no! She was alarmed. *They're either going to rescue me and take me home or they're going to run me over!*

Before anything could happen, the river split up into three different pathways. "Which one should I take?" She looked hopefully at each choice. "I want to make the right decision!"

"Captain," a voice cried out from the massive frigate. "which way are we taking?"

"Steer to the center," she heard a gruff voice respond.

"Guess I'm not going that way." She steered to the left -- it was closer anyway. But soon after changing course, the river started to get rockier and the ride became bumpier. The raft started to slow down and finally came to rest. When she stood up, the raft cracked in two and tipped on its side. When Iyaa stepped onto the other half of the raft, it tipped and took her over the waterfall.

"Ahhhhhh!!" she screamed. As she fell all she could think about was her grave in front of her dad's house. She hit the water face first. She swam with all her might, but water seemed to slap her with full force no matter which direction she went. She felt powerless as the current swept her along. *Where's the raft?* The water was moving too fast for her to see anything.
It's no use... I'm going to die here!

She was exhausted and ready to give up when she noticed that the current had slowed down and was actually moving her towards the bank. She looked around, trying to figure out what her next move should be when she saw what looked like blue ice. *Wait a minute!*

Her eyes widened to catch sight of the blue ice again, but it moved away. She swam as hard as she could and finally caught up with it. Just as she reached for the stone, passed out. The river carried her limp body downstream, finally depositing it on the bank of a wide bend. Iyaa lay still, but the sun caught a glimpse of the blue stone shining between her fingers

~~~~~~

As usual, Darclep was worried about something. "Yeks, can you telepath Iyaa?" he asked.

"Sure." Yeks closed his eyes. They suddenly popped open again, wide with fear. "We have to find that girl quickly. I don't know what happened to her!"

"Yeks, you stay here with Ashin," Darclep ordered. "Doshan, you're coming with me."

Doshan reluctantly went with Darclep and sailed into the sky.

~~~~~~

Not a word was spoken when Ashin and Yeks were alone. Ashin glared at him and stepped back. *I'm not going to talk to that murderer! He killed my dad. I know it. I know it!*

As if feeling the loathing emanating from Ashin, Yeks grimaced, then went inside the tent to lie down, while Ashin chose a spot the bare ground about three yards away and sat down.

"How many have we found?" he asked himself. He pressed his hand against his forehead, trying to remember. "Three." He felt totally fatigued. "This is taking a very long time... too long."

~~~~~~

For the second time, Veil tinkered with the diamond jewel. To many people's eyes it was a stone, but in her opinion, jewels are pure, not contaminated with filth, especially inside of them!" Right before her eyes, the stone was transformed into a rigid sword. Veil ran to her master.

"My lord?" Veil gave her lowest bow, her head practically touching her knees. She waited for permission to rise.

"What is it, Veil?" the master snapped.

"Please be patient, my master." Veil trembled in fear.

"Patient? Patient? Why should I be patient with you?" the Annihilator roared. "I still don't have all seven of those jewels, you asinine Wabhyc!"

A loud gagging and choking sound was heard, then the words, "Please, my master, spare me." A loud thud followed, which meant something or "someone" had been thrown on the floor.

"I'll give you one more chance -- one more week. If the jewels aren't here by then, you and Yeks will die!"

~~~~~~

The news quickly got to Yeks. He was worried and it showed in his physical features. His hair looked gray instead of white. He looked like a living dead man every time he walked. His wrinkles looked deeper than ever. *We're not going to be able to find the jewels in time!*

8

Silence wrapped around Darclep's and Doshan's tongues. Darclep looked at Doshan as they glided through the sky, but Doshan didn't look back.

Darclep sighed. "Look, I'm very sorry about what happened when there was an Underground Biracial Juveniles with Powers club."

"What happened to it?" Doshan said flatly. He still made no eye contact.

"The old members died," Darclep replied, swallowing a lump in his throat. Darclep felt like he'd died, too, as if the golden arrow Ashin found represented the death of everybody that was involved in the UBJP. Somebody may as well as carved "R.I.P. UBJP members" on the stones that were used as the entrance in and out of the UBJP headquarters.

"That's okay." Doshan said. Darclep looked at him, confused. Doshan rolled his eyes. "You said 'sorry' -- remember?"

"Oh yeah," Darclep chuckled.

Nothing else was said as they traveled above the Ceoxdra River as the clouds tried to catch up with the faster-than-a-millisecond winged boys. Forests were hidden under blankets of snow. There were no boats were in the water as the river and lakes were frozen solid.

The boys stopped and settled onto the ground when they saw the river split into three different channels. "What path do you think we should take?" Doshan asked Darclep.

"I don't know. I think she'd take the one in the middle."

"No! She's not like other girls, not even a normal child for that matter. 'Lunatic' is a much better word for her. I believe she took the left."

"No! That one has a waterfa--" Darclep paused, then grinned a sly grin. "Might as well not sit here bragging about how right I was!"

The were off, soon hovering over the river and swooping down the waterfall that was now one gigantic icicle, a deadly dagger ready to tear up anybody who walked beneath it. They both floated down and went different directions, scouring the area for signs of the girl.

Doshan started off at the riverbank of the river. It was early morning, the sun hadn't come up yet. Doshan was looking for something black in the snow. He came to the end of the path on the left side of the river, about ten yards away from the waterfall, where he met up with Darclep.

"Did you find her?"

"No." Darclep's tone said it all. He felt like he'd failed. One of their group had already died because of him. It was about to be two.

"Stop worrying, Darclep," Doshan said. It was as if he read Darclep's mind, but instead he read his attitude. "We'll keep looking."

When the sun peeked over the horizon, Doshan and Darclep resumed their search. As Doshan was coming back from the middle of the waterfall to the end of the river, he noticed that some of the snow was grayish. He brushed away the snow and uncovered a face with black skin. He pulled the person out of the snow and noticed it was Iyaa, the gossipy little devil!

A murky blue stone fell out of her hand. Doshan smiled and as he reached down to grab it, he felt another hand -- not his own -- grab his arm and squeeze tightly. Iyaa opened her eyes and glared fiercely at him. She kicked him in the stomach, forcing him to the ground, then stomped her feet on his wings.

"Ow! Stop it!"

"Take it back!" she shouted.

Doshan was perplexed. "Take what back?"

"Give me the jewel and take back your words!" she snarled.

It suddenly occurred to him what she meant -- he had forgotten that she could telepath!

"I've got to be more careful around her," he mumbled.

Darclep came running towards them. "Thank The Creator, you're alive!"

Iyaa just nodded, but continued to glare at Doshan, as if a warning. Soon they were off, soaring towards Baltham and the Omni Mountains.

~~~~~~

That night, when the sky looked most black, with only a drop of blue for color, white eyes were seen outside of the coal-black volcano. The sky glistened from the weeping clouds. It smelled of midnight mist. Still pouring, the freezing rain could numb a face with only a few drops. "Tip. Tap a tap. Tip. Tap a tap," it repeated, warning people to go home -- stay away or be caught in a flood.

The eyes swept around Karcickel Valley as her moose hide sandals became muddier by the second. *Yeks, where are you?*

Veil, you woke me up from an awesome sleep! What do you want?

How many have you found?

We found another one today...so now we have four.

One more to go, then... this is easier than I expected.

No chopped heads, eh?! Yeks chuckled. A mumble was heard in the telepathy. *Hello? Veil, are you still there?*

102

I'm here. She interrupted him. *We still have one more to go. Find it quick!*

The conversation ended with that last command.

~~~~~~

"What is that white number eight on your left hand?" Ashin asked between bites of a roll smeared with applebutter.

"It's how I keep track of how many wishes I have left of the ten," Iyaa answered, loosening the wrapped around her swollen ankle so she could limp over to get some food.

"I thought you'd only used one?" Yeks joined in the conversation.

"No, I used two." She said flatly. Everybody waited for a better explanation. She sighed in exasperation. "Wabhycs are supposed to use the wishes only when Death is coming our way. I was going to freeze to death, so I wished for warmth."

"Oh," everyone chorused.

Darclep pulled a dagger from his bag and gave it to Yeks. Iyaa got a bow and arrow. Ashin also got a dagger and Doshan got a bow and arrow similar to Iyaa's. "Just in case," was all he said.

"Where did you get these?" Ashin asked.

"Made 'em."

They walked on a path in the Omni Mountains. The paths split into two branches -- left and right. "I believe it's the left path to the other side of the mountain," Iyaa said, but Doshan disagreed, "I believe it's the right path to the other side of the mountain."

Darclep sat between both paths. He flew up to the sky to see where the paths ended. When he was satisfied, he levitated back down. "Let's take the right path," he commanded.

"Who made you king?" Iyaa hissed. Darclep ignored her, so Iyaa went the opposite way.

"Where are you going?" Doshan called after her. Doshan could tell the girl was very spoiled.

"I don't believe your way is right," she said calmly, crossing her arms across her chest.
Ashin glanced at the Iyaa, noticing that she was holding something in her hand. He cleared his throat, then went over and stood beside her. "I'm going her way," he said to Darclep.

Now Darclep was boiling mad. "I'm not lying to you! I would never do that!"

Ashin tried to keep a serious face on. "I know." He thrust Iyaa's hand into view.

"She's not either."

Yeks was confused. "So there are two ways to get to the other side?"

Ashin was amused that they didn't understand. "Don't you get it? She knows where the other stone is!"

Darclep rolled his eyes and went straight towards the two nine year-olds. Doshan and Yeks followed. While they followed Iyaa, Ashin whispered to her, "Use your powers... for what they're supposed to be used."

"I really don't know how tired you are of this crazy trip, but you don't know how tired I am. And just to let you know, I'd rather be dead than listen to your crazy advice!" she responded.

They were finally in front of their destination. Ashin clutched his dagger, wondering, *What will be in this place?* It was a cave and smelled of rotten eggs and lemons. It was quiet except for a rubbing noise. Nothing except a dark shining object was seen. The texture was made from rough rigid walls of rock. The spirit of the room made Ashin feel unwelcome.

"I really do think we should go--"

Iyaa widened her eyes and shook her head slowly, mockingly. She shivered a fake shiver and Ashin glared at her.

"Iyaa--" Darclep let out a warning signal.

"Oh, I see I've got company," they heard a voice say from inside.

Everyone pulled out their weapon. They were ready for anything -- or they thought they were anyway. Out slithered a foot-long slimy snake. Iyaa pulled out her bow and arrow and shot at the snake.

"I've been waiting for this moment for a long time!" said the snake.

The snake's eyes turned black and he grew longer and fatter. Everyone charged at it. Yeks and Ashin stabbed it. Ashin's knife turned into a black liquid and Yeks turned to rock. Iyaa tried to run inside, but the snake tripped her. Darclep tried to have his Balthamian force bring her out of the cave, but it was as if the snake had Balthamian powers because Iyaa couldn't be budged! Darclep took a few steps back and shot one of the arrows into the heart of the vicious beast. The snake was now as tall as Omni's highest peak. It shot out venom, but Darclep dodged it. Then Iyaa tried to get out, but the force always brought her back into the cave. Doshan thought of an idea. *I hope this works.*

"Darclep, Ashin, Yeks -- don't fight this thing. Just stay still!"

They obeyed his orders, but the snake was still growing bigger! Doshan looked at Iyaa and she smirked at him.

"Can you listen?" Doshan yelled.

"You didn't mention my--"

"This is no time to play games! Please, just do it!"

Iyaa shook her head. "Then you leave me no choice!" Doshan electrocuted her.

"Noooooooooooo!" the snake screamed. It was shrinking to its regular size and then it froze into a statue. Darclep and Doshan carried Iyaa out of the cave. "We need to electrocute her more often!" Doshan chuckled. Darclep nodded and watched Ashin and Yeks get out of the cave unharmed.

"Look, it's a garnet!" Yeks called out.

Darclep grabbed it and put it in the bag. While Iyaa recovered from her state of shock, they walked out of the light blue, snow-capped mountains.

The seven slowly faded away to a six on Iyaa's hand. She gripped her hand as if an evil spirit had walked through her mind.

"Where is it?" Ashin asked.

"Where is what?" Iyaa responded. Everyone was either staring or glaring at her.

"Okay, okay." She gave in. "The two jewels are in one place. That place is… Htevaon."

Everyone gasped except for Yeks. He started to play in his long beard. The wrinkles on his face started to look like ridges made from the aftermath of an earthquake or like the core of a ball shrinks while the skin does too, but not properly.

"Yeks, what's wrong with you?" Darclep questioned.

"Nothing," he said quickly. "Nothing at all."

Doshan flew and picked up Iyaa, the brat. Yeks flew alone and Darclep picked up Ashin.

During the whole trip to Htevaon, Yeks hardly said a word. The wind started to war full force with the falling snow. It was a miracle. Doshan was able to kill a deer for food during their horrible weather. A fire was made, but was quickly blown out. Everyone slept uncomfortably that night.

~~~~~~

Veil sat by the window of her room. As she looked out, a tear rolled down her cheek. She was remembering the times she was free from the chains that held her in bondage. Even though she worked here, there was still a "you better do it, or else" attitude. "It's too late though," she whispered.

Veil looked away. She had work to do and plans to make. A heart full of ice and stone shouldn't melt, but it could. The sad thing was, Veil wouldn't let it.

~~~~~~

That morning, they awoke to a soggy, wet ground. Yeks shook everyone up.

"Wake up before you catch cold."

Slowly, but surely, everyone got up and began to walk towards the border. They ate venison along the way, which gave them some energy to continue the journey. Yeks' corrugated skin puckered slightly around his lips as he nervously ran to the border and, sure enough, made it there first.

Veil, we're at the border.

Good. I'm outside of Htevaon.

Okay, bye.

Iyaa's spine began to feel frozen. Sparks flew from her hair until the tips were on fire. Her eyes turned red. *Something bad is happening or is going to happen,* she telepathed to everyone around her. As they passed Karckikel valley, the flowers began to wilt. Everything began to darken except for the sky. It started to get sultry and the air was dry and brittle as they got closer to Htevaon. There was a bubbling, boiling noise heard. From far away, piercing, ghostly screams could be heard. The kids looked at each other. Finally, they made it to the front of Htevaon. A hooded Wabhyc stood in front of them. The Wabhyc took their hood off. "Akizha esimo. Udmmne shiyeno."

"Cailati meyetto."

"Eishaka cayYekko!" the lady chanted.

Mud started to pile up into hills that transformed into people. Yeks disappeared into the sky as he chanted something to make clouds come together and get darker and darker. "This storm is going to be better than the one I made a few years ago!" he shouted with glee.

It's the real Yeks! Ashin screamed in his mind.

Darclep and Doshan flew up in the air to find and fight Yeks. The Mudmen grabbed Ashin, but he made fire bolts and cooked them.

"Hello, my daughter."

Iyaa's eyes and hair turned back to normal. She took a few steps back. "Mom?" Iyaa's voice was trembling.

Yeks fell to the ground and Ashin ran to fight him.

"I can't believe you, liar and murderer!" Ashin lunged at him. "That's for my dad! I'm going to tear you to pieces!" The fight was on.

"Cayena!" Yeks called out. One of the Mudmen melted into quicksand and Yeks threw Ashin in it.

"Somebody help me!" shouted Ashin. Darclep rushed to Ashin, but surprisingly, lightning struck Darclep and he dropped the stones. Yeks grabbed the bag of stones. Until he was inside, Yeks made the lightning zap Darclep, Ashin, and Doshan every time they made a move.

"Nooooo!" Ashin was so angry he started to hate himself for letting Yeks go, but there was nothing he could do. The quicksand was to his shoulders. "Somebody help me!" Ashin yelled with all his might. *I haven't even grown up yet. Please don't do this to me!*

Darclep, wake up! You need to save Ashin. I'm busy! Iyaa telepathed him.

"Zeefereh!" Veil roared. Iyaa was suddenly frozen. *My daughter, you should give up! You're going to die!* Veil telepathed.

You know what? Iyaa snapped. *I'm not related to you. A parent will always be there for you. A parent would never leave their child wondering if the puzzle of their heart and life is put together when you threw all of it away!* Iyaa melted herself with the heat in her body.

110

Veil's eyebrows crossed. *No mercy!* she growled.

You're playin' my game! Iyaa smirked. Her hair flamed up again and her eyes turned back to red. *The name's not' daughter,' it's Iyaa. As I say to everyone, 'You're going down!'*

"Hah!" Veil snorted. "You can't do this alone!"

"I know," Iyaa smirked, looking at Ashin, Darclep, and Doshan sneaking up behind her mom.

Veil screamed a scream that would make the whole world deaf as she fell to her own death. A cobra appeared, bit her, and said, "Come join The Annihilator and become his real slave for the rest of your death!" Veil became transparent and followed like a zombie. Out of her hand fell a diamond and a quartz. Yeks levitated those jewels and threw them into the lava of Htevaon.

"Why do you have to give us a hard time?" Iyaa screamed. "Doshan, fly me up to the top of Htevaon!"

Doshan shook his head. "No, you could get killed!"

"Are you one big fat chicken? Get me up there!" Doshan swooped down to get her and flew her at the top of Htevaon. "Drop me."

"No! Are you crazy?" he said.

Drop me!

Her thought transfer startled him and he dropped her. The stone continued to sink in, as she dived into the lava. Iyaa was nowhere to be found in that sweltering hot bubbling swirl of yellow, orange, and red. Finally, her head bobbed out the lava and she threw out the stones. Lava leaped over her head and her arms battled against the waves of lava. She bobbed her head once more, attempting to climb out and cough up something before the lava consumed her.

"Oh, no... no!" Doshan yelled. "She's gone! Dead!"

"She can't be dead!" yelled Ashin, running toward the volcano. He climbed the coal-black rocks and fell a steeple's fall. Salty tears streamed down his cheeks.

"The lava is like water to her," Doshan mourned, "but she's drowned by now. Her ankle might have weighed her down. She is more than dead."

"Nooo!" Ashin bawled.

A bald eagle came out of the entrance of Htevaon. It gripped a bag in its talons. It set the bag beside Ashin and bowed. Ashin looked inside.

"Thanks!" Ashin said genuinely.

"No problem," the eagle answered as it transformed into a human male.

9

"**W**ho are you?" Ashin inquired.

"My name is Aglee." Aglee pointed to the dove next to him. "This is my wife, Vodea."

The dove on the ground evolved into a beautiful, fair-headed woman. She curtsied in her white silk dress. "Pleased to meet you," she whispered.

"Well, we have to be off!" Aglee's smile was like rays of sunlight. Aglee softly gripped Ashin's shoulders. Vodea turned into a bird and flew away. Doshan and Darclep flew with their own wings.

"Where are we going?" Ashin asked.

"I'm going to take you to see who wrote the letter!" Aglee chirped.

Everyone flew in lightning speed. If you walked from Htevaon to the place they were going it would take up to a year! Finally, they came upon the golden mountain. Everybody had to shield their eyes from the mountain's brightness, but they got used to it in no time. They entered Sacrejhon and saw it was as bright on the inside as it was on the outside.

"Behold, The Creator of all!"

Everyone bowed for they were unworthy to see him.

"Get up, my dear ones," he said. "As I have promised, you will see the face of who sent the letter, for I sent it."

When Ashin got up and looked the Creator in the eye, he saw every race inside of him.

"Come here, my son."

Ashin wanted to say no, that he was not his real father, but then he remembered his dream. "Dad!" Ashin said, running towards him. When he hugged the Creator, it felt like hugging a soft, warm pillow on a bitter frosty day.

"Come, my sons."

Darclep and Doshan ran up to him.

The kids saw seven golden chairs embedded with diamonds to the right of The Creator's throne. "These are the seats for the favored ones when they pass away," he informed them. "May I see the stones?"

Ashin gave him the jewels. The Creator put the topaz on the second chair; the garnet on the third; the ruby on the fourth; the emerald on the fifth; the quartz on the sixth; and the sapphire on the seventh.

"Why didn't you put the diamond on one of the chairs?" Ashin asked.

"Because I need you to see it first." He handed it to Ashin. "Flip it over."

He flipped it over and saw that his name was engraved on the murky straight diamond that was carved into a sword. Ashin was close to tears. "Why are all of the jewels murky on the inside or dirty on the outside?" Ashin asked.

"You know part of that answer. They don't believe me."

Ashin closed his eyes. *I believe in The Creator and from now on, until the day I die, I will,* he thought with all of his heart.

He opened his eyes and saw the diamond jewel shine before his own eyes. He put his hand on the boy's neck and his sword birthmark came off and was on the Creator's palm. He pulled at the royal purple handle and when he pulled it from his palm, it became a real sword. He handed the sword to Ashin.

"It has always belonged to you."

Ashin nodded and said, "Thank you."

He did the same for the others' birthmarks. "As for all of you, I have something."

The Creator pulled out three crowns. "Ashin, I crown you King of Xarnynthia. Doshan, you are King of

Faristana. Darclep, I crown you king of Baltham. Tell them The Creator commanded."

"Kids, do you want to hear something?" Aglee asked as they flew out of Sacrejhon and landed on the ground.

"What?" Darclep replied.

"I'm the one who sent the note."

The kids gasped and each of them unwrapped a smile on their face for a short second.
"I did it when everybody went outside. The girl looked at me because she was on the tree, too and thought I was a regular bird!"

"Cool," Ashin mumbled. He clenched his teeth and swallowed the lump in his throat.

"I just wanted you all to know that," he said before he flew back to Sacrejhon.

"I don't know how to describe this odyssey… Adventurous? Funny? Bittersweet? Maybe all of them all together," Ashin said, speaking a little louder than a whisper.

"Maybe a life lesson…" Doshan chided. They finally landed in the country of fire.

Darclep cleared his throat. "I've decided I'm going to close down the Underground Biracial Juveniles with Powers."

"I agree." Doshan concurred.

"Okay," Ashin spoke, "but let's keep the tunnels and stuff. We could just invite everyone instead of keeping it a secret." Darclep nodded.

"Then it's settled."

Everyone joined in a last UBJP-first-time-as-friends group hug, then they went their separate ways.

Ashin's stomach churned like the fresh butter his mom used to make. Ashin inhaled all of the smells: something always burning, fresh baked loaves of bread made from the bakery nearby, raw meat, and spoiled fruits. It had been more than a few months since he'd been back to Soclid.

He thought about the recent trip he made, how it unveiled his true selfish self and how prideful he was, how he needs to watch his mouth. He learned what a real friend is and how one should act.

"I hope I threw all of my old self away," Ashin worried. Ashin took his crown off and hid it behind his back as he neared the big house. Like Doshan said, there was a grave. Swallowing it was a rainbow of flowers. Ashin gulped the lump down his throat. "I hope my family will accept me." He knocked softly on the door.

"Who is it?" A voice called out. Someone opened the door. The man's eyes widened and his mouth dropped when he saw who it was. "Is it really you?"

Ashin nodded. "Hi, Uncle Eter," he mumbled in exhaustion. Eter hugged the boy until Ashin practically suffocated, then Eter slapped him on his bottom. "Don't you ever do that again! You understand me?" His red eyes filled up with tears of concern. "We thought you were dead," he whispered, sobbing.

"I know," was Ashin's short response.

"Mayla, there's someone here to see you!" Eter winked at Ashin and left the room.

Mayla briskly walked to the door. She put her hands over her mouth when she recognized the boy whose top layer of hair was red. She swooned and Ashin chuckled at the sight.

He went into his room and slept for the rest of the day. No one was in his dream, only colors. It was as if red and brown were fighting. There were times red defeated brown and times brown defeated red. The dream that went red only had a little to go.

"You know the end," he heard a voice say.

"Ashin! Ashin! Ashin…Ashin, are you awake?" Ashin's eyes were only opened to slits, but he knew who it was.

"Mom!" He hugged, well, practically squeezed her tightly.

"I'm glad you're back," said Mayla.

"Me, too."

"May I ask you something?"

"Sure!"

"Why did you leave?"

Ashin told his mom everything. He told her about Doshan first taking him to UBJP and how he came home late that same night. He told her about Iyaa's "drop-in" and Doshan getting kicked out. He didn't forget to mention the mysterious letter. He went on about their first adventure with the spider and what happened to Rief. He told about all of the deaths, including Iyaa's, and everybody they met. By the end of the day, his mom knew everything he went through.

"So, you met him and he said that?"

"Yes, and I have proof." Ashin turned the back of his neck towards his mom to show her his birthmark was not there; then, he got the sword and she gasped.

"It looks exactly like your birthmark!"

"It is."

"Well, we have to leave for Xarynthia immediately and go to your own peo--"

"Oh, mom--" he interrupted.

"What?"

"Why did we go to Soclid?"

"You hardly had an outlet to use your powers!"

Ashin and his mom hugged again, then there was a deep silence.

"I was thinking about punishing you," Mayla started off, "but I believe you went through enough with the deaths of people who were close to you then you went to Htevaon. It's a good thing you didn't meet the Master of Death himself! There will be many-a-time when I should punish you, but this one isn't one of them."

Ashin looked at the floor. Even through clenched teeth, a tiny smile managed to slither all over his face.

Mayla sighed. "I saw that. Right about now, let's enjoy your "Welcome Back Home" feast."

"What kind of food are we having?" Ashin inquired as his mom led him out of his room.

"Venison and vegetable stew, fresh baked bread that Lya, Doshan's mom made, and your favorite fruit drink -- pear juice. I hope you don't mind, but I invited Iyaa's dad to the party."

"I don't mind," Ashin said flatly.

They walked into the dining room. "Surprise!" The word rang all over the big house.

Ashin jumped and his eyes widened with happiness. Everybody he knew was there: Everyone in the Big House, Darclep's family, Doshan's family...and Iyaa's dad. There was an empty seat between Darclep and Doshan.

"Are you being punished?" Ashin asked.

Doshan leaned back in his chair and smiled. "Not even close!"

"I got off squeaky clean!" Darclep declared boastfully.

They all fell into an uncontrollable fit of laughter.

"Come on, everybody, let's hold hands!" Qana announced.

"Mighty Creator," Savov began with his eyes closed, "we thank you for this food, but most of all, we thank you for bringing Ashin home safely. Amen."

Everyone chattered in several different conversations as they ate. Ashin shifted his eyes from left to right. He didn't feel right. He squirmed as he was talking to everyone.

"Wait just one second." Ashin got out of his chair, walked over to his mom, and whispered something to her.

Mayla looked at him. "That's very thoughtful of you, Ashin. Go in your room, do what you have to do, and I'll go tell everyone else."

Ashin ran to his room and changed. He met up with all of his guests and the residents of the big house outside. Ashin and his guests picked many flowers. They walked single file to the Nyen Forest. Ashin was first in line. They stopped at the gray boulder used to enter the tunnel and Ashin put his flowers on top of it. *We miss you, Iyaa.*

~~~~~~

"I don't know why I hired you!" the Annihilator thundered.

"I tried, my lord."

In this setting in Htevaon, all you could do is use your hearing. "You hardly used your powers to defeat those young kids!"

"I'm sorry."

"They're kids!"

"Please don't kill me, Master," Yeks begged, trembling.

"You leave me no choice!" he roared. A deadly moan was heard and then everything was quiet. A body was thrown out and if you look closely before the cobras appear you will see who the dead body was. I don't even have to tell you.

You know who.

www.ingramcontent.com/pod-product-compliance
Lightning Source LLC
Chambersburg PA
CBHW050829180626
46814CB00004B/1522